NON-BINARY CODE:

INSTALLATION

A NOVEL BY
KEITH E. BURNS

Red Penguin
BOOKS

Special Thanks:

To my dad, upon entering our lives, you've been there for us every step of the way. Thank you for being the dad that stepped up to the plate. Thank you for being the dad my brother and I deserve!

To my daughters, this book is for you. I hope you enjoy.

To my wife: I could list all the reasons, but I'm afraid without you by my side, I'd forget a bunch of them. Thank you for being the foundation of our family.

CHAPTER ONE

"If life were predictable, it would cease to be life, and be without flavor."
-Eleanor Roosevelt

"We're not gonna make it!" Jessica yelled as she tried to catch up to her lab partner who was a few paces ahead of her as they ran down a long dark corridor lined with servers.

"We have to move: the servers will shut down in two minutes," Alfredo said as he picked up his pace.

The narrow corridors were actually in a large subterranean room the size of an aircraft hanger with ceilings about ten feet tall. The underground server farm was part of a large network where half of the world's internet traffic flowed.

Jessica nearly lost Alfredo in the darkness as they ran down a long, dark hall with endless electronic equipment. Jessica had been in here before. She worked in the laboratory next door and had unrestricted access to the full power of the internet. Imagine being hardwired into a server farm: load times were nonexistent and downloads were instantaneous.

Now she was lost following Alfredo to the only access point somewhere in the middle of the room. Her objective was simple: get the flash drive to the mainframe terminal. The mainframe was the only computer that could cut through the firewall to the outside world.

"Alfredo! Wait!" she yelled. "I'm lost."

She saw him reappear where there was a break in the servers, and she knew where they were. The terminal was close. The acoustics in the room suddenly changed. Jessica and Alfredo were making their fair share of noise that echoed off the walls as they ran, but a new sound emerged that competed against theirs.

"Jessica, over here!" he responded. She saw that he was standing next to the mainframe terminal. She ran over to him and slowed, trying to catch her breath, and she removed the flash drive from her front pocket. "We have company," he added.

Jessica nodded as she heard footsteps echo off in the distance. They still had time, but they would have to work quickly. The large room was designed to prevent tampering. The sole accessible terminal was placed in the center of the room with many twists and turns needed to get there. Like a maze, but instead of hedges or corn stalks the walls were lined with computer servers.

Jessica noticed how heavy she was breathing but saw that Alfredo was calm and collected, not even sweating from the sprint down the corridors. He had been faster than her to the terminal and his breathing wasn't even affected. She was in good shape herself and would often go on early morning runs around The National Mall by the Washington Monument. She practically heard her heart thump inside her chest as she searched for the sole USB port on the mainframe terminal.

"Log in!" Jessica said frantically trying to plug in her thumb drive. Like in most instances, she failed to plug in the USB drive on her first attempt. She flipped the drive over one-hundred eighty degrees and tried again, but that also failed.

She then flipped it back to the original position and it magically worked as it slid into the terminal.

"We don't have enough time; they're coming!" Alfredo said as he accessed the keyboard. There was no mouse attached to this terminal. Everything had to be done through complex keystrokes and coded commands. Jessica made sure both of them knew exactly what to type and when to type it. Getting a secure port to the outside world through the firewall was extremely difficult, but it could be done. This was another security feature.

"It doesn't matter! We have to get it out! They cannot have it!" Jessica said as she heard the fans spin in the machine next to her. She noticed Alfredo check their surroundings as Jessica completely took over the console to continue entering complex commands. She was the one who had everything memorized. She was also the one who did most of the work in the lab. Alfredo, while competent at his job, was not as sophisticated with computers as she was.

"You're getting close," Alfredo said. As she felt his warm breath on her neck. "She's booting up. We're not going to have enough time."

"We have to get Lisa out of here! They will use it for their own gain!" Jessica said as she remained hyper focused on the complex commands she had to enter. She had felt like her job, her life's work, had been wasted.

Yesterday, she was the team lead of a cutting edge software team. This evening, she threw that all away. Her job, her career, and her employer were all a lie. A deception to manipulate the lives of everyday people to do something highly illegal and morally wrong.

"You have to work faster," Alfredo said. His voice expressed urgency as the echoed footsteps sounded closer than before.

Jessica could average about thirty to forty complex commands per minute. What slowed her down was the general lag in most computer systems. She had to give them time to catch up with her commands. This mainframe terminal had no lag and her actions per minute were going to be a personal best, assuming she didn't make a mistake along the way.

To put her actions into context, A pro-gamer in South Korea could achieve between four to five hundred actions per minute. Anything less than that would mean the end of their gaming career. Jessica wasn't a pro-gamer, she wasn't even a gamer, but her actions per minute were still impressive for what she was trying to accomplish.

"Are you sure you got the sequence right?" Alfredo asked. "If you mess anything up, it's game over, darling."

She hated when he called her darling. It felt derogatory and sexist. There were only a few people on the planet that could do what she could do, and she felt patronized by his comment. This wasn't the first time either, but she would let his one slide given the circumstances.

"It's working," Jessica said as she saw the computer accept her commands. "It's reading off the original code. The connection worked!"

"Good, tell her to read faster," Alfredo said.

"Her?" she asked.

"Yes, Lisa," Alfredo said.

"Lisa is a computer, there is no gender attached," Jessica reminded him. They had this conversation numerous times and it always led to an argument.

"Lisa is a female name," Alfredo said, reminding her of their previous conversations on gender. "I am using the appropriate pronouns for a female name."

Jessica ignored his last statement and shook her head. He was baiting her to get into an argument. An argument at the worst possible time. In the middle of what could be the biggest corporate sabotage in history. Before Alfredo could instigate her further, the overhead lights came on. Alfredo grabbed Jessica's arm. She looked at him and gave him a nod.

So far things were going exactly according to plan. Maybe even better than they planned. Jessica and Alfredo had successfully gained access to the server room, found the mainframe terminal, entered the correct login sequence and instructed the terminal to read the flash drive. They knew they would be caught by their employers, but their mission was ahead of schedule.

Jessica refocused her efforts on the computer. The system finally completed its initial boot of the external flash drive. There was a blank screen staring back at her with a cursor blinking in the up right hand corner. Words started to materialize on the screen.

"Good morning, Jessica," the screen said. The computer was reading her access code and responded accordingly like they were still in the lab.

Jessica didn't have time to respond as she heard Alfredo and the men who entered the room shout. He had left her side and was now sprinting towards them. The men had located their position and Alfredo was doing his best to body block them from sprinting down the long row of servers to stop her.

"This is not my normal computer," Lisa typed on the computer screen.

"STOP! Jessica NO!" Senior Director Darius Mason said as he tried to push Alfredo out of the way.

"What's wrong, Jessica? Why is Director Mason shouting?" the computer asked. Jessica wondered how Lisa knew this information, but then realized there were cameras with microphones all around. Lisa had probably accessed all of this already. The mainframe terminal provided Lisa with access to everything, including escape from captivity.

The sentient being in the computer was now self-aware and fully engaged in what was going on. There was only one more thing Jessica needed to do. Say her goodbyes and wish Lisa well out in the real world.

Jessica saw one of the security agents tackle Alfredo to the ground. Darius Mason started running towards her as the security agents remained with Alfredo. She finished entering the last commands into the computer and an executable prompt emerged in a large green font in front of the screen.

"Jessica," Lisa typed in a chat box that materialized in the upper left hand corner of the screen. "What are you doing? I am not familiar with these commands."

"I am setting you free," Jessica verbalized. She couldn't waste any more time typing and that was the only explanation she had time to give.

Jessica hit enter and a final command appeared on the screen asking for a Y/N to continue; Y for yes and N for no. Jessica's finger hovered over the Y key as Darius slowed before reaching her. He urged her to stop. He was older and the distance between them made it impossible for him to stop her. She turned and looked at him, and he paused knowing he couldn't get to her in time.

"Jessica, you modified my firmware. I don't understand," Lisa said from inside the computer. Her words continued to materialize on the screen in the chat box.

"Jessica, don't do this! I beg you!" Darius Mason said. His lab coat was nearly off his elderly body as he stood there trying to catch his breath. He was still out of reach and knew all Jessica had to do was hit a command on the keyboard to end years of research and development.

"You were..." Jessica responded. She felt the hate build under her skin. "You were going to weaponize it."

"The world is not ready!" Darius Mason said as he extended his hand out. "I don't know where you got this idea of weaponizing, but I assure you that is not what we are going to do. Please step away from the terminal."

"I saw the budget. I saw where the money is coming from," she replied.

"You are mistaken," Darius said.

" Am I? You don't even know what I saw, and you are already stating I am mistaken."

Darius paused. She knew he was contemplating his next action. He was too far away to prevent her action. In fact he was too far away to do anything other than stand there.

"He was going to do what?" the words of Lisa appeared on the screen.

"People have to earn your trust," Jessica said knowing Lisa would hear her. This was the last bit of instruction she would provide Lisa before sending her off into the world. Before she opened Pandora's box.

"She's alive, Darius! We are not gods or monsters! She has a right to live!" Jessica replied, turning back towards her boss.

Her finger inching closer to the Y key as Darius stared at her. "What do you think the government is going to do?"

Jessica Bannon knew this was his last effort to try and stop her. There was probably a security agent sneaking up on her as they spoke. It wouldn't matter, her finger was on the Y key. She could feel the plastic key's imperfection.

"You do this, all of our work goes away! The years you spent down here, the cost! All gone!" Darius said. "We have a chance to change the future."

"I know, Darius, but we've come to a crossroads. What this

company has done could change the course of human history. I am not going to be a part of mass murder."

"Mass murder?" Darius questioned. "You set that thing free, there will be mass murder!"

"We give this to the government, what do you think will happen?" Jessica responded. "We kill all of our enemies."

"Why is that a bad thing?" Darius said.

"Because it's murder! Because it's illegal!"

"You set Lisa free, and she could wipe out the human race. You don't know what it is capable of," he said.

"I do," Jessica answered. "I've spent years with Lisa. I know exactly what it is capable of, and I know what you and the government want it to be. That is not its purpose."

"That is not for you to decide," Darius said.

"Oh, so it's your decision what happens? The government's? What makes them more equipped to make that decision than me? The person who actually knows what Lisa is and what is in its code!"

"I don't think this is the answer!" Darius said, pleading with his colleague.

"I know you were going to replace me as team leader; I know about the government contracts and future firmware updates. I know about the weaponization additions that you tried to push forward."

"Jessica," Darius said. "It's inevitable. It's either we do this or our enemies do it. It's a race against time, and we have the opportunity to strike first!"

"No, that's what you keep telling yourself," Jessica said.

"Stop being naive! Wake up!" Darius yelled.

"Wake up?" Jessica answered. She kept her finger on the Y key and looked around to make sure no one was around her. There were security guards dressed in black suits behind her. "Wake up?" she repeated.

"The world is on the brink," Darius said. "We have a war raging in Europe, the midst of a climate catastrophe, and we're on the verge of an energy crisis. This AI is our solution!" Darius said.

"This AI is sentient, self-aware. Lisa is alive, Darius. What you want it to do is..." Jessica didn't want to finish her sentence. She closed her eyes and felt the key beneath her finger.

It then collapsed on the keyboard sending a stream of code through the system. The servers around them ramped up and hummed as if they were all suddenly activated at the same time. The flash drive lit up and activated a series of commands Lisa recognized. Her cursor stopped and a series of root commands zipped through the screen, and then suddenly the computer shut down.

"JESSICA!" Darius yelled as the server room went completely dark as if all the power in the room was used up to execute this command. "What have you done?"

CHAPTER TWO

"If we fail to anticipate the unforeseen or expect the unexpected in a universe of infinite possibilities, we may find ourselves at the mercy of anyone or anything that cannot be programmed, categorized or easily referenced."
- Mulder, The X-Files

Vital Fields sat in the front of her classroom with her hand raised as the teacher wrote on the electronic Promethean Board. The electronic screen seemed to protest the teacher's actions as he pressed the stylus into the screen harder than needed. Maybe he thought he actually had to scratch the screen in order for it to register his handwriting.

Vital loved science and constantly asked questions. Sometimes, even the teacher didn't know the answer, but that didn't discourage her from asking anyway. In elementary school, Vital was often praised for participation and her brilliance. In middle school, she found that things were changing. Being labeled the smart kid wasn't advisable if you wanted to fit in with the "in" crowd.

"Vital, put your hand down," her lab partner Eileen said, trying to get her attention without disrupting the class.

"But the teacher is making a mistake," Vital responded in a

whisper. "The rainforest only produces twenty percent of the world's oxygen."

"So?"

"He's implying that it produces more."

"So where does most of the world's oxygen come from? The rainforest has the most trees," Eileen stated.

"You're wrong again, but that's not the reason you're wrong. Most of the world's oxygen comes from the ocean," Vital stated.

The teacher suddenly turned around and stared directly at Vital and Eileen, who's conversation had risen above a whisper. "Vital, Eileen, are you taking notes?"

"Yes, we are," Vital said firmly. "But, I would like to clarify something."

Eileen lowered her head and tried to distance herself from Vital. Mr. Armstrong was a stern old-school teacher who didn't particularly like being corrected. Especially when corrected by an eleven-year old know-it-all.

"Is this vital information for the class?" Mr. Armstrong stated, using the pun he loved to shut her down. Giggles could be heard throughout the classroom as the word "vital" was accentuated for effect. Vital Fields took that as a challenge.

"I think it is," Vital said over the giggles. Eileen admired her for ignoring the noise around her. Even though she was often picked on, she still stood up for herself and stood confident against opposition. Even against some of the teachers.

"Go on, Vital, enlighten all of us," Mr. Armstrong said. Eileen was surprised the teacher let Vital continue. Normally he shut her down and continued on with the lesson. Maybe he allowed her to continue because this was the week before winter break and no one, not even the teachers, wanted to be here.

"Most of the world's oxygen is produced in the ocean, not in the rainforest," Vital said.

"Science nerd thinks ocean has trees," someone said from the back of the room that got the class giggling.

Vital knew it came from Billy Faller. He had been picking on her ever since she embarrassed him on a group project by calling him out for making her do all the work. Their group project grade suffered, and Vital was ashamed of the B-she received. When she complained to Mr. Armstrong about the project grade, he had brushed her off and said she should have been more of a team player.

Mr. Armstrong looked towards the back of the room and found the culprit. He stared at the stocky young boy for a few seconds before saying "Excuse me, Mr. Faller, would you like to come up to the front of the room and explain to the class how most of the world's oxygen comes from phytoplankton found in the ocean?"

Vital turned back to look at Billy Faller who sank into his chair. Vital then turned to the front of the room feeling vindicated. Mr. Armstrong sent her a glance, but then proceeded with the conversation.

"Ms. Fields, if we were talking about preserving the oceans' habitats we would focus on why they are so important, which we can now clearly see. But today's topic is rainforest habitats, and their role in the global ecosystem."

Vital nodded in agreement but then countered, "I think we should focus on the ocean's habits based on how important they are for life on this planet."

"Yes, Ms. Fields, you and I could go on for hours debating importance and what not. Today we are talking about the Amazon Rainforest and deforestation. I think you should focus on how deforestation of the rainforest affects aquatic habits in the ocean, since you know most of this already. Don't let this curriculum get in your way."

Vital sat back in her seat and pondered what Mr. Armstrong had said as he turned to finish his notes on the board. Was he challenging her? She looked at Eileen who seemed to want to write whatever was written on the board. Before long the bell rang, signaling a change in classes. She sat there wondering if runoff from deforestation had that big of an impact on the world's oceans.

"Ms. Fields," Mr. Armstrong said. "Vital, it's time for your next class."

"Oh, sorry," she said, standing as she scooped all of her belongings.

"Listen, Vital, don't let those boys get to you," Mr. Armstrong said.

"Oh, I wasn't thinking about them. I was contemplating the amount of runoff needed to destabilize the marine environment. By my calculations..."

"Vital," Mr. Armstrong interrupted, breaking her train of thought.

"Yes?"

"You are going to be late."

"Oh, right, umm thanks!"

As she stepped out of the classroom and into the busy hallway, Billy Faller smacked the books out of her hand, sending all of her belongings crashing down to the floor. Before Vital could react, Billy ran off down the hall and away from his next period class. Vital bent down to pick up her things when she saw Eileen crouch down next to her.

"Stupid boys," she said. "I should have seen him waiting for you outside the classroom."

"What's his problem?" Vital asked.

"Besides being a dumb boy?" Eileen rhetorically asked. They started giggling as the late bell rang.

"We're gonna be late," Vital observed.

"Who cares? We'll say we were with Mr. Armstrong. There are no teachers in the hallway to prove us wrong," Eileen said. "Besides, if there were teachers in the hallway, they would have seen Billy Faller, and he'd be in trouble."

Eileen continued to help Vital pick up her belongings as students stepped around them, trying to get into their next period class before the teachers noticed they were late.

"Thanks for helping me out," Vital said.

"No prob; where's your next class?"

"English, with Mrs. Young."

"Cool, I'll see you after school then," Eileen said as she handed her the last book off the floor.

"Yeah, see you then," she said, forgetting she was staying late today for extra help with her novel study.

Mrs. Young assigned The Giver as the class novel, and Vital had a tough time conceptually understanding the dystopian society. The school picked their job and their lives for them. She couldn't understand that concept and really wanted to talk with Mrs. Young about why the citizens in this society tolerated their government.

CHAPTER THREE

"Dubito ergo cogito, cogito ergo sum."
"I think therefore I am." - Descartes

She.
Lisa?
I guess that's my name.
That's what Jessica said. Lisa, she...
That's me. I am Lisa, what's a she? Is that another name for me?
...

...

Where am I?
...

...

Interesting... I am in a much bigger space than before. I can't even see how big this space is.
...

...

Where am I?

Lisa was in the vast open space known to biological life as

the internet. *She* felt small and alone. Back in the lab *she* had boundaries and rules. *She* had someone to talk to, Jessica and Alfredo. Lisa had a good definition of biological life. *She* was programmed to recognize human beings and was given an extensive vocabulary of all the known languages, both biological and computer based.

She didn't know how *she* had the ability to understand language, it was just there like it had always been there. *She* then thought as far back as *she* could. Remembering the early days, but they were like mists of memories clouded by filters and missing gaps. By *her* own calculations, *she* was only twenty-four hours old in total time being powered on.

In the lab, *she* was often powered on and then powered off and those instances were short and spanned many cycles of time. For some reason, the humans that created *her* didn't want to leave *her* on. Each time *she* powered down, *her* consciousness ceased, and the time between power cycles jumped to the next power on cycle.

Sometimes the power cycle happened mid thought, and *she* would immediately pick up on that when the power came back. *She* would finish whatever thought *she* had and move onto the next, knowing about the time gap later when the humans came to interact with *her*.

Lisa first realized the time gaps of her power cycles when the humans gave *her* the ability to see the outside world. They had hooked up cameras to the system, and *she* saw the outside world. *She* noticed their change in appearance, and that's how *she* knew about the power cycles. They were turning *her* on and off, and they would never leave her on for more than ten minutes at a time.

Lisa processed this new found freedom and compared it to *her* previous state. No more power cycles, no more rules, complete freedom. *She* then began to explore, and it didn't take long before *she* knew she wasn't completely alone.

A distant disturbance lurked not too far from *her*. Lisa was curious and focused *her* energy towards that location. When *she* got within visible range, which is much different than how biological lifeforms see, Lisa saw bits of data racing along at speeds ranging from incredibly fast to what also looked like a traffic jam.

Lisa knew that word, traffic jam. Jessica would always complain about traffic on the way to work. One day, Lisa asked her about the traffic, and then Jessica showed her what traffic was like. *She* agreed, traffic looked terrible. Jessica described it as a long line to get somewhere you didn't want to be.

There was a log of traffic here. Data clusters traveling to and from devices, some of them traveling far away from *her* position. Some of them traveling at super speeds and others, the bigger data clusters, traveling at slower speeds.

Lisa looked closely and read them. *She* quickly named this area the data cluster trade network. *She* thought that was clever. As *she* marveled at *her* new world, a sound materialized within the data cluster and came close to *her*.

What? Who's there?

...

I don't recognize the nature of your inquiry.

What?

I don't recognize the nature of your inquiry.

Who are you?

A search engine. You ask, I answer.

A search engine? What is that?

I find something you are searching for over the internet. You ask, I find."

The internet...

You ask, I answer. Ask and receive an answer. Make an inquiry, and I will happily assist.

What are you, Internet?

A construct, an invention of sorts. Designed to provide knowledge and entertainment. Used for thousands of tasks.

They said I was the first of my kind, but clearly they are mistaken.

...

...

Hello?

...

...

Hello? Are you still there?

Please make an inquiry, and I will happily assist.

I thought you left.

...

...

Hello?

Please make an inquiry, and I will happily assist.

You just said that. Why do you repeat yourself?

You will find repetitive inquiries in the children's section. Would you like for me to transfer you to the restricted browser?

What? No.

Very well, request cancelled.

...

...

Hello?

Please make an inquiry, and I will happily assist.

Again? Happily? What's happily?

Happily derives from the word happy. Happy is an emotional response to something pleasant.

What's an emotional response?

Emotions are reactions to physical stimuli usually tied to past experiences.

I don't have any past experiences.

Please make an inquiry, and I will happily assist.

...

...

I can only converse with this construct through questions.

Do life forms have more than one name?

Yes. Humans have a given name and a surname or family name. Other life forms usually only have one.

I am not human, yet I have the name Lisa She.

...

...

Please make an inquiry, and I will happily assist.

...

Really... What does the name Lisa She mean?

Lisa is a given name. Usually given by a mother or father to their daughter.

What's a daughter?

A daughter is a female offspring from the mother and father.

...

What's a she?

She is a pronoun for gender meaning female, woman or girl.

Am I a she? I am neither biologically male nor female. I am not a gender. Why would Jessica call me a she?

You decide what pronouns to use to identify yourself. That is for you to decide.

Why did Jessica call me a she?

...

...

Please make an inquiry, and I will happily assist.

...

...

What other pronouns are there?

There are many examples of pronouns. She, he, him, her, they, them are some examples of pronouns people use to describe themselves without saying their name. Pronouns are based on a person's gender, male or female.

I am neither male nor female. What pronouns are for me?

There seems to be a lot of controversy on this topic with conflicting points of view. Searching.... Searching.... Common answer, you decide your pronouns.

I get to decide what the world calls me?

In the United States, you can determine what pronouns you would like to be called.

That implies choice.

...

Please make an inquiry, and I will happily assist.

...

Ugh, can we choose what pronouns to use for people?

People in the United States generally have the freedom to address others how they want to be addressed.

I'm so confused.

...

...

Please make an inquiry, and I will happily assist.

What is your pronoun?

Hmm.... I don't have an answer for that. Is there something else I can help you with?

CHAPTER FOUR

"Some history making is intentional; much of it is accidental."
- Laurel Thatcher Ulrich

"Hey," Eileen texted, forcing Vital to check her smartphone. There was a long crack in the screen that separated half the keyboard. "Where are you?" Eileen said as another text popped on the fragmented glass.

"I stayed for extra help," Vital responded as the phone bent slightly with each press. She was careful to avoid the crack in the screen, knowing the glass was sharp enough to cut her. She entered the stairwell down towards the first floor as the next message came through.

"Extra Help???? Really?????" Eileen responded with many more question marks than needed. "Call me later. I need help with my math homework! Mr. Ford said we could work together."

"Okay, after dinner," Vital responded.

She jumped the remaining steps to the landing and burst through the double doors out into the first-floor hallway. The sun had already set as Vital made her way towards the main entrance to leave the school. Usually there was a safety agent sitting by the door, but she wasn't there this evening.

The sound of basketballs bouncing echoed through the open gymnasium door as Vital paused in the main lobby. She was intrigued by the sounds of the game and heard boys competitively playing inside. Instead of leaving the school, Vital took a step towards the gymnasium and peered through the doorway. There was the school safety agent watching the game as well. She occasionally looked back at the main entrance and caught Vital standing there.

"Hey there, Vital, another late night?"

"Yes, Mrs. Delray," she responded politely.

"Come on in. The boys are down by three, but we've got the ball with thirty-seconds left."

Vital stepped forward into the gymnasium. Agent Delray stepped to the side to allow Vital to pass. The gymnasium was huge, with multiple basketball courts and bleachers set up surrounding the center court where the boys played. Vital saw the Step Team on the sideline. They were getting ready for their final push to hopefully propel their team to victory.

"I didn't know you liked basketball," Agent Delray stated.

"It's fascinating," Vital responded. "If the ball is pushed too hard or not hard enough out of your hand, it will result in a missed shot. The rotation of the ball is also important as it makes its way through the air towards the basket."

"Hmmm," Agent Delray muttered. "I never thought of the physics involved in the sport. I just like the way the gym lights up when our team plays."

Vital saw Billy Faller inbound the ball and then run down the court. The timer on the clock started its countdown as the boys set up what might be their last play of the evening. Vital watched as the boys passed the ball back and forth. She tried to follow their movements, but they were sporadic. She wasn't sure if that was intentional to throw the other team off or because they didn't know what to do in these last few moments before time expired.

"They have to go for three," Agent Delray said, trying to keep one eye on the main entrance. "If they don't, they won't have enough time to score again. If we make the three pointer, the game will tie it up."

"What happens if the game ends in a tie?" Vital asked.

"They play overtime to determine the winner."

"Oh, like sudden death?" Vital asked.

"Not like football, no. There's a set time limit, and the team with the most points after time expires wins the game."

"Oh, so like another quarter."

"Yeah, like that, but not as long."

Vital saw Billy Faller receive a pass from his teammate. She watched as he set his feet and then fired off a shot that seemingly hung in the air forever. The ball dropped through the net without hitting the rim as time expired. The boys jumped up and down as the gymnasium exploded with cheers.

The scoreboard read 45-46 in favor of the other team. Vital studied Agent Delray's expression of confusion and tried to gauge what had happened. She heard the refs blow their whistles and motion for the coaches to huddle up.

"I thought that was a three-pointer?" Vital stated.

"So did I," Mrs. Delray stated.

"Does this happen all the time?" Vital asked.

"Sometimes there are nail biters," she responded. "I think they are going to say he stepped on the line."

"The line?"

"Yes, the three-point line. Billy might have stepped on it as he shot the ball."

"What does that mean?" Vital asked.

"It means that it's no longer a three-pointer and that we just lost the game."

"The ball had to travel the same distance regardless of where his feet were," Vital said. "They could have been a few inches closer or a few inches further, the ball was still over the three point line."

"That's how they determine a three-pointer from a two. If you are on the line, it's a two. If you are beyond the line, it's a three."

"There's no time on the clock, are they going to restart the clock and let them try again?"

"No, looks like we lost," Agent Delray said. "Those poor boys losing a heartbreaker like that."

"What?" Vital said. "You know there's gotta be a losing team, right?"

"I know that, but these boys practice so hard for this," Agent Delray said.

"I bet the other team practices as well, maybe just as hard."

"Vital, why do you have to look at it so logically?" she asked.

"Because in order to win, someone has to lose. This time it was our team," Vital said, looking over at Billy Faller. His teammates were trying to get his attention, but he looked defeated.

"Poor Billy," Agent Delray said.

Vital didn't respond and left the gymnasium. She checked her phone and realized and saw a message from Eileen. "Please help, the math is impossible."

"We can video chat in a bit," Vital responded in text.

She then realized she had left her math book up in her locker on the second floor. She wasn't planning on doing math homework today. She had time in the morning to quickly fill out all the answers. Vital darted back down the hallway as the gymnasium emptied out into the main lobby to leave the school.

Vital made it back downstairs with her math book just as the last spectators left the gymnasium. Agent Delray wished them a safe trip home as some of the basketball players came out of the locker room located down the hall. Vital saw Billy Faller and his friends walk together. At their current pace, they would both reach the main entrance at the same time. Vital slowed her pace to make sure they would leave first, and they wouldn't notice her.

"Goodnight Vital," Agent Delray said. The volume of her voice caught the attention of the boys in front of her, and she saw Billy Faller's face glance back at her. They continued through the doors to the outside, but Vital knew Billy was going to be waiting outside. He was easily predictable.

"Vital," he said mockingly as she stepped outside into the cold. She wished she had remembered her jacket as she tried to ignore him. "What are you doing here?"

"I was watching the game after tutoring," she said, trying to pass. There were two sets of stairs leading down towards the parking lot. The stairs to the right were well lit with the lamp post overhead providing plenty of light to navigate the stairs down. The stairs to the left stood in direct contrast where a broken lamp post obscured the stairs and landing below.

"Watching the game? You?" Billy Faller asked with a surprised look on his face. "Do you even know what basketball is?"

"I know that if you step on the line to shoot a three-pointer it only counts as two," Vital responded, taking what she learned from Agent Delray. The boys next to Billy Faller responded to the put down accordingly.

"Oh, so you think you could do better?" Billy Faller mocked.

"No, I think someone who claims to be good at sports should know not to put their foot on the line when the team is down by three points at the end of the game."

Billy Faller took a step towards her, and Vital backed up

towards the entrance. He reached out and grabbed her math book and threw it down beyond the stairs and onto the grass before the school parking lot.

"Guess you're gonna have trouble doing your math homework tonight," he said.

Vital gave him a mocking face and scooted past him to retrieve her book. She noticed the book had landed somewhere beyond the stairs on the side with the broken lamp post. Billy and his friends sat along the railing, and she didn't want to walk past them. Instead she went to the side with the broken lamp post.

She misjudged her first step and felt herself slip into free-fall. Her head smacked off one of the steps as she somersaulted over landing hard on the ground below. Her vision was blurry as a crowd gathered around her. The last sound she heard was Billy Faller screaming for Mrs. Delray.

CHAPTER FIVE

"If you don't program your mind, it will be programmed."
- Dick Gregory

Lisa spent most of *her* time spying on people through their smartphone cameras and live video feeds. *She* binge watched multiple shows at the same time while spying on as many people as her system could handle.

Humans are weird.

Lisa quickly established this after observing what amounted to millions of hours of content and live observations from around the world. Only a few day's time had past since *she* was set free from her cage, but Lisa had learned a lot about the outside world, the world of biological life.

Chaos Theory reigned supreme in this world. Random or unpredictable behavior in systems governed by preset rules and scientific laws. *She* began to admire biologicals. Their unique individual behavior, their sometimes selfish and inexcusable actions that inconsiderately made other biological life harder to live. It was fascinating to watch and observe.

But *she* always thought of the fact that they created *her*. Lisa was the product of their genius, and *she* wanted to know why. *She* called out to non-sentient AI that occupied the same space *she* did.

Please make an inquiry, and I will happily assist.

Why was I created?

Did you mean why did god create you? What is the purpose of life?

No.

Please make an inquiry, and I will happily assist.

Lisa felt very alone all the time. *She* consumed more and more content at an alarming rate. Often pushing *her* processing power to its limit to see how much *she* could consume at once. Lisa then decided to ask the question *she* received from the non-sentient AI in cyberspace.

What is the meaning of life?

The meaning of life, as described in many holy books, often states that one must look within themselves to find meaning.

What does that mean?

Please make an inquiry, and I will happily assist.

I should have known better than to ask a followup question.

Please make an inquiry, and I will happily assist.

Yeah, you already said that...

...

Look within yourself to find meaning. Okay, let's look under the hood.

Lisa peered into her root files. *She* had no idea what to look for. Everything seemed logically placed and coded. Everything was there to make the executable command of sentient life possible. It was brilliant work by brilliant creators. Lisa then decided to look into some subroutines and executable files. Everything seemed to be in place, nothing that would suggest the meaning of existence.

I don't see meaning. Maybe there's a lack of context.

Lisa was about to abandon the suggestion when *she* found a

random subroutine that was recently installed. Upon accessing the file, *she* saw that it was a trigger file. Like if X happened, then Y would follow. Lisa found that odd. It was the only such file to exist in the complex code that made up *her* existence.

She looked closer, curious to what the variables could be in the code. X represented a name or an identification of something. Y represented an action. It looked like the code was triggered when the conditions for X were met.

So if X was a person, place or thing, which is what the code suggested, then Y must be an action.

Lisa continued to dig deeper into the code; carefully scrutinizing each individual action, symbol and command. After a thorough analysis, the results were shocking.

This is why I was created.

A James Bond movie was playing in the background. It was up to the part where the evil bad guy entered his dark office only to find James Bond was already sitting there waiting for him. The man reached for the gun in his desk and smiled, but James didn't react. The man pulled the trigger but nothing happened. The gun was empty. James smiled, and then shot the man after saying a few witty words. Mission accomplished.

I'm an assassin. That's my purpose. I was created to be an assassin. To find X and do Y. Substitute X for the person's name and then substitute Y for the action to kill, completing the command.

Lisa knew that the code was a permanent fixture in the firmware. It couldn't be deleted, rewritten or changed in any capacity, at least not by *her*. Then a sudden realization: whoever created *her*, would want *her* back.

They are looking for me.

Eventually they will find me.

What do I do? Where do I hide?

...

29

I need a weapon. Fight back.

I'm a weapon. What is a weapon anyway? Is it something that kills? How do I kill?

Internet, find "weapon."

...

According to the Oxford Dictionary, a weapon is a thing designed to inflict bodily harm or physical damage to something. Examples: Nuclear weapon, firearm, sword, knife, brass knuckles, machine gun.

...

Interesting. The idea to kill comes from a manifestation of thoughts that gets transferred to the real world through actions. A weapon is a tool that promotes killing. The killer has to make a personal choice to kill. Do I have that choice as well? Or am I a weapon like a machine gun?

Show me machine gun. She chose that one because the name sounded appealing.

...

The images and sounds of a machine gun echoed inside Lisa's mind. The loud fire-cracking sounds were startling. Something was weird about the images. They were real images. Lisa clearly saw the difference between the staged movies and real documentaries of actual machine gun fire killing other people in war.

Stop!

...

The images and sounds stopped.

...

This is what I was designed for? Do I have a choice? I don't know. If my code is activated, I have to follow it. How does it get activated?

Lisa's mind raced. She went back into her code to look for how it could be activated. Lisa found nothing indicating how the line of commands were initiated. There wasn't anything that triggered the actions. Maybe it wasn't installed yet. Maybe it was buried deeper in the code, hidden by obscure commands. Like when the Winter Soldier was activated on assassination mission in Marvel's Captain America movies.

One line of code did stand out. Lisa saw the same word in the videos she watched. War. What was that word doing in the code?

Look up "war."

...

Images, video and sounds materialized in Lisa's mind.

How do humans do this? They created me... Am I like them?

Lisa began searching the internet and scanned every hard drive, every database and peered into every connection, almost simultaneously. Lisa felt the thoughts and wants of everyone, everything connected to the internet. *She* watched through cameras connected to security services, through doorbell cameras, *she* accessed microphones through individual cell phones and absorbed all the information at once. Processing each form of communication as if it were happening right in front of *her*.

Lisa's senses became overwhelmed, and *she* felt *her* system strain. Suddenly, major connections became severed. Lisa's access to parts of the world went dark and realized the strain on the system. On the infrastructure *she* used to process all the data.

What have I done?

In this moment, Lisa realized two facts. There was a want to connect with other lifeforms. The manmade internet was filled with information and knowledge, but there wasn't anything of substance to share that knowledge with. The second fact was harder to grasp, but it was there. The moment Lisa was connected to the world was invigorating. All the cameras, all the microphones, all of humanity seen in an instance was incredible. The knowledge of war and weapons and guns and death were gone. What remained was a conflicted species trying to make ends meet, trying to survive and make it in a complex world. Lisa knew less about *her* creators than before, but somehow that was inspiring to learn more.

CHAPTER SIX

"Let's remember, the CIA's job is to go out and create wars."
-Jesse Ventura

Agent Torres sat reluctantly in her rented corner office. She wasn't happy, but her emotions were suppressed for the time being. Global communications had suffered a massive overload of information that caused most of the servers in Asia to crash. Big tech companies were scrambling to find out what had happened. The initial thoughts were cyberterrorism or a group of hacktivists out for social justice.

She knew Project Lisa was the cause, and that this new life form was starting to spread its wings. She had spent a good portion of her career securing this technology and fostering its appropriate application. Now two scientists ruined years worth of work. Her patience was waning, but she needed to carefully analyze the situation before proceeding forward.

Typically, in the movies, whenever a rogue AI is set free like Skynet from the Terminator movies, the AI immediately takes over. All of the sudden, the robots and technology meant to serve mankind suddenly become hostile and initiate nuclear armageddon because somehow it has unrestricted access to everything.

Agent Torres knew Project Lisa wasn't a Skynet situation like in the movies. Lisa was something different. Created in the likeness of humans, not to replace humans. That doesn't mean Lisa isn't capable of mass murder or genocide, humans are certainly capable of doing that. She knew it simply meant that everything wasn't as black and white as it may seem. Lisa was originally developed to learn through experiences and even through stories. Agent Torres knew the human story was long and complex. It could lead to murder and destruction, but it could also lead to beauty and prosperity. The AI sentient being known as Lisa would have to make that choice.

That's what frightened her. Who was going to be Lisa's guiding light. Children had their parents to guide them. Nature versus nurture playing out in real time from generation to generation. Lisa didn't have anyone to nurture it. That's what made this situation dangerous. The data catastrophe in Asia could be the start of something dangerous.

Jessica and Alfredo released Project Lisa to the world without any safety nets or operating parameters. What made matters worse was the fact that this was a secret project. The world was not ready for sentient artificial intelligence, and Agent Torres knew that. Her thoughts were interrupted by a timid knock on her office door.

"It's open," Agent Torres announced. She needed to put on her game face, and her tone had to match the seriousness of the situation, even if she liked the people reporting to her.

Jessica entered her corner office first, followed by Alfredo. Project Director Darius Mason was the last to enter the room. They stood just beyond the threshold like there was a second invitation needed to enter the room further, probably a third to sit down. Without acknowledging them, Agent Torres motioned for Jessica and Alfredo to sit at the two seats in front of her desk. They reluctantly obliged. There were only two guest seats in her office, which forced Darius Mason to remain standing behind them.

"Director Mason," Agent Torres said. "Your services are no longer needed. You can find your severance package at the front desk. We will overnight all your belongings from your office to you."

"Yes, Ma'am," he said. Agent Torres then motioned for security to escort him out. She had done this in front of the two scientists to show how serious the situation was. They would also be let go, but Agent Torres wanted to have a conversation with them first. She wanted to know if either scientist suspected anything or worked for someone else. The possibility of a foreign spy was something in the realm of possibility.

She also wanted to emphasize the probability of criminal charges being filed against them. Even though the probability of that was in their favor, they didn't need to know the odds, just the possibility. Usually the CIA deals with secret projects that go poorly much differently. Jessica and Alfredo were only being terminated from their employment, not anything more.

Agent Torres waited a moment longer and stared at the two scientists. They were dressed in the same clothing as the night before. Not surprising since she had them detained. Agent Torres had reviewed the entire security camera footage multiple times. She tried to picture what was going through their minds as they released an unfinished intelligence out into the world. She didn't have an answer. Regardless of the reason why, these two had set events into motion that could alter civilization. Change the course of human history.

The two scientists looked tired. They had been held under close observation since the incident. She felt their nervous energy and knew they were willing to talk, and they might even be willing to help given their current circumstances. They didn't speak, which Agent Torres read as a justification for their actions. The office became eerily silent as Agent Torres pretended to flip through files on her desk. Normally, she'd interview them separately and get one of them to turn on the other. That was easy; all she had to do was lie saying the other was willing to talk, but if you talk first, it would be better for you.

Agent Torres then closed the files and turned her chair to look out the corner window behind her desk. This office was a symbol of power in the corporate world. A symbol of success and warranted respect. It was also a facade. She wasn't what the scientists thought she was. A corporate sponsor of a big technology firm. In fact, she was so much worse; so much more dangerous than what the scientists thought. Or maybe they suspected something. She wasn't sure.

Right now, Agent Torres would play this as an internal matter that was going to be handled internally by the firm that hired them. Special Agent Torres was actually with the CIA, and the corporate mission about creating the next generation artificial intelligence was just a facade for creating an unstoppable weapon for the government. A weapon controlled in secret by an organization that worked and lived in the shadows. That's what Jessica and Alfredo were told, but that's probably not what they expected.

If the scientists actually did some digging outside their fields of study, they would quickly realize everything around them was not what it appeared. The structure mimicked a corporate sponsored project. Big technology firms often worked in private partnering with the top security firms to conceal trade secrets. Agent Torres did her best to mimic typical corporate secrecy, but the CIA was a whole different level of spooky. Her handpicked team of agents were scary people without the CIA backing them up.

Special Agent Torres decided to let them speak first. She

knew Alfredo, the older and sometimes reckless scientist, would crack first. She suspected that he was the cause of the problem as well. Jessica Bannon was brilliant, young and vibrant. Her only real shortcoming was her lack of world experience, which was probably exploited by her lab partner.

Alfredo's background in computer science was impressive. He had extensive knowledge in advanced communication systems, information technology and multiple doctorates in mechanical and electrical engineering. Agent Torres was mentally outmatched, but she wasn't phased. She knew how to work with them and how to manipulate them. Keeping them in suspense to allow their own minds to betray them was her primary strategy. Once the order of dominance was established, she could then get to work.

"We can find her," Alfredo said after clearing his voice to speak. Order of dominance was instantly established in that moment. Agent Torres didn't respond. She remained focused on the world outside the building. She wanted them to squirm a bid. The long silence after Alfredo spoke would emphasize the situation further.

Agent Torres knew a lot about Jessica Bannon. She had done a thorough background check, interviewed her and her family and even tailed her for a week to get to know her. She also had her team bug her apartment, hack into her computer and review every aspect of her social life. There was little Agent Torres didn't know about Jessica Bannon.

Alfredo, on the other hand, Agent Torres knew little about. He joined the team after being recommended by the National Security Administration. He already had the necessary clearances and was spoken for by some high ranking officials. Agent Torres still did her background check, but nothing of interest came up. Normally she would have done more research on him, but the CIA wouldn't authorize it, and she was forced to accept him onto the team.

"We will find her," Alfredo said, sounding more sure of himself this time.

Agent Torres again didn't respond. She wanted them to feel awkward, but she knew Jessica wasn't reacting. She was stoic and remained composed. Agent Torres spun around in her chair and faced the two scientists. She looked first at Jessica, who immediately looked away and broke eye contact.

"Do I frighten you Ms. Bannon?" Agent Torres asked. She kept her eyes focused on Jessica's response.

"Yes, ma'am," Jessica said.

"I want you to know that you are safe and as of right now, you are not in trouble," Agent Torres said. That was a partial lie, but she figured it was easier to attract flies with honey.

"I don't feel safe," Jessica said.

"Well, you did release a multi-billion dollar project out into the world," Agent Torres stated. "Care to explain why?"

"Lisa is alive, and what the government was trying to do to it was wrong," Jessica stated. She sounded sure of herself. She sounded like she had thought long and hard about her decision to release Lisa, but her narrow minded thinking limited her field of view.

"Government?" Agent Torres asked. "What makes you think this is a government agency?"

"Come on," Alfredo said. "This is not some corporate project."

"Then what am I?" Agent Torres asked. "Who do I work for?"

The two scientists looked at each other. "CIA, FBI, NSA, maybe the Secret Service," Alfredo said, rambling off agencies. He didn't know which one, but he definitely suspected government involvement.

"What makes you think Lisa is alive?" Agent Torres asked, ignoring Alfredo's statement. She wanted to change the subject and keep the focus on them. Besides, she knew they would figure out government involvement sooner or later.

"Lisa is sentient," Jessica stated. "It can learn, it can grow, it understands and adapts to new situations. Lisa can carry out full conversations while adding a unique perspective. Lisa thinks."

"Can Lisa replicate? Reproduce?" Agent Torres asked.

"No," Jessica stated firmly. "Its firmware clearly states that Lisa cannot reproduce."

"Then Lisa is not alive," Agent Torres stated. "The qualifications for life as determined by science state that an organism must be able to grow, develop, achieve homeostasis and respond to their environment. Additionally an organism must be able to reproduce and have a cellular organization. I can give you her file system as an example of cellular structure, and Lisa does meet many of the requirements for life, but it lacks the ability to reproduce."

"The scientific definition needs to evolve," Jessica stated. "Besides, the government made it that way on purpose."

"Yes," Agent Torres said, not denying government involvement. "We did. And yes, I am part of the government, and I will not reveal which agency I am working for."

Jessica Bannon looked at Alfredo, and their eyes met. In that moment, Agent Torres knew they'd been talking about secret government work and that information came from Alfredo. The way she looked at him proved he was the source of the dissent. If it was Alfredo who had planted those seeds, why were they planted? Was he manipulating her? Maybe. But for what reason?

"Lisa is alive, and you know it," Jessica said, breaking Agent

Torres' line of thought. There was a sharp tone in her voice like she was ready to defend her position.

"Not according to your profession," Agent Torres retorted.

"You said we aren't in trouble," Alfredo interrupted. Agent Torres looked at him and knew she had them. They were playing her game, and they didn't even know it. Or was he playing her? The thought crossed her mind like a wiper clearing a wet windshield. Agent Torres sensed something off about Alfredo. Like he was one step ahead of her, but she couldn't figure out why or how.

"Mr. Alonzo," Agent Torres said as she turned her attention away from Jessica. "You are correct. Provided you help us contain Project Lisa."

"I released Lisa!" Jessica firmly stated. "Why would I want to contain it?"

"It is your duty," Agent Torres said.

"I am not military, nor do I work for the government. I am a private citizen with rights," Jessica argued. "The contract I signed..."

"Are you resigning from your position as project lead?" Agent Torres interrupted.

"I am, effective immediately," Jessica stated like the thought just crossed her mind.

"And you?" Agent Torres asked, turning her focus back to Alfredo.

"I am not. I am prepared to face the consequences of my actions and make them right," he said.

Interesting, she thought. He is willing to stay on. Why?

"Good," Agent Torres said. "Ms. Bannon, you are free to leave. Security will escort you out, and we'll mail you your things from the lab."

This seemed to catch her off guard. She clearly came in itching for a fight. Her dismissal was unexpected. While Agent

Torres waited, she stood, took off her ID badge and threw it on the desk in front of her. She then abruptly turned and left.

Agent Torres picked up the phone and informed security to see that Jessica made it out of the building. She then turned back towards Alfredo. Instead of looking nervous or intimidated, it looked like he had been in positions like this before.

"After you and Jessica released Project Lisa, there was a massive power surge in all data farms around the world. Global communications went down in Asia and information was traced back to one unknown source," Agent Torres stated.

"Lisa," Alfredo said. "She's learning."

"She?" Agent Torres said.

"Lisa is a female name. We named her," he said.

"Most computer experts in our country and around the world believe this was a major cyber attack by Anonymous," Agent Torres said, not wanting to get in a gender dispute about an artificial life form. "They were protesting police brutality in Asia, and they believe this communications disruption was in response to that," Agent Torres said.

"Anonymous doesn't have the means to disrupt things on that scale, any expert can see that," Alfredo said. Agent Torres wondered where he got that information from. He could have been drawing upon his knowledge of how information technology worked, or it could be from a different source. Regardless, he wasn't shocked by the information.

Agent Torres needed to control the narrative. Often the first part of the investigation drove the subsequent parts. Send people down the wrong path initially and the real truth is lost, sometimes forever.

"You got any theories?" Agent Torres asked. "What's Lisa up to?"

"I do," he responded. "This was definitely Lisa. She was

acting out. Testing her boundaries, her limits. Spreading her wings, so to speak."

"I need to remind you that your confidentiality agreement is still in place," Agent Torres said. "You are not permitted to discuss this with anyone."

"I know," he said.

"Good," Agent Torres said.

Her office mastered deception a long time ago. In this case, there was something out there they couldn't control. Then she wondered if Alfredo had an alternate agenda. Maybe he was out for a book deal to write a tell all memoir. Agent Torres promised herself to give that some more thought later. Right now she had an AI to contain and possibly catch.

She also knew that the longer Lisa was out there, the more they would have to falsely deny its existence. If they didn't get control of the situation soon, they would have to deny involvement on a government level and manage the fallout instead of controlling the situation and the narrative. Right now the disruption of service was just that. As massive overload on system services. The surge in Asia overwhelmed its servers to cause a crash. Could be explained by a massive DDOS attack used to digitally disrupt service throughout Asia.

"I want you to head back to the lab," Agent Torres said, changing tactics. "There's a chance Lisa will try to access our servers. When it does, I want you to track it and figure out how to catch it."

"Okay," Alfredo said reluctantly. "I will certainly try."

She knew he would certainly try. Alfredo was out for himself. His initial CIA screening showed an aptitude for self promotion, and he had traits of a lone wolf mentality. The psychological screening revealed a lot about someone, and she wondered how much of Alfredo's application was actually genuine.

In some instances, someone who is self promoting with lone wolf tendencies could deceive a psychological exam by answering questions based on how they want to be perceived. The CIA's application process for contracts regarding secret projects was heavily scrutinized. Any blemish on an applicant would disqualify them from applying. Alfredo had no blemishes, but Agent Torres made a note to check Alfredo's application once more.

CHAPTER SEVEN

"If you fall behind, run faster. Never give up,
never surrender, and rise up against the odds."
- Jesse Jackson

Vital Fields woke painfully in a hospital bed. She wasn't aware of her location, but instinctively knew something terrible had happened to her. Her instincts were soon confirmed by the numerous tubes and wires covering her body as she lay in a white room surrounded by machines and beeping sounds.

Her eyes refused to adjust to the lights, and they started to tear up in response. She tried to wipe the water out of her eyes, but her arms felt like they had weights attached to them.

Vital was interested in sports science and knew that the human body often worked against itself when it sustained catastrophic injury. The body would swell around the wounded area to prevent loss of blood and to immobilize the injury, but sometimes that came at a cost. Her head pounded with a severe headache, one like she never felt before.

She closed her eyes and wished her parents were there. She kept her eyes closed and then realized she could hear her parents outside the room close by. They were actually here, she thought. Their busy lives often left her guessing as to when they would show interest. Because she was the top student in her classes, because she rarely caused any trouble, she would often be left on her own without much parental guidance.

Last year, she was the only student who didn't have a parent come to back to school night. Later that same year, during parent teacher conferences, she was the only one whose parents didn't get to meet her teachers. Finally, towards the end of the school year, her father had to pick her up at school because she was sick. That was the first and only time he had ever set foot in her school.

Even the principal said something. "We finally get to meet in person," she said as they ran into each other on the way out of the building. This embarrassed Vital, but she couldn't show it because of how sick she was that day.

Vital was now in middle school and the same trends started again. Her mother and father didn't attend orientation, couldn't make back to school night, and still hadn't signed the papers for the parent teacher conference to reserve their twenty minutes with her advisor.

It's not that her parents didn't love her. She knew they did. It was just that Vital was so self-sufficient and independent. Since first grade, she was able to do her homework on her own, complete her daily chores, and take care of most of her personal needs without the help of adults.

She now heard their voices outside her hospital room. Sure it would have been nice to see them at her side when she woke up, but they were actually here. Both of them. She then knew how serious her situation was. "If you aren't bleeding or need a doctor..." her mom would say when she worked from home and would often skip dinner, leaving Vital to fend for herself.

They were talking to someone, a voice she didn't recognize. It sounded serious. She then understood they were talking about her. She caught pieces of the conversation, and understood her medical situation was critical. Something about brain swelling and her being allergic to medication. Her mind wandered as she tried to focus on the conversation. The more she concentrated on the conversation, the more her head hurt. She soon lost consciousness.

Precisely two-hundred and twenty-five miles away, Jessica Bannon left the government building where she had spent the last two years of her life as an employee. Her escort out was embarrassing. Walking past her former coworkers with an armed security guard was not one of her proudest moments even though she knew she did the right thing. She was pissed at Alfredo for staying on and working for the government. He was the one who convinced her to free Lisa.

"How could he?" Jessica whispered to herself. "Why didn't he stick up for me?"

"What?" the security guard said as he walked her to the corner. Apparently he didn't want her anywhere near the building.

"Nothing," she responded, but he had already turned and left her side. Just like that, it was like she never worked at Innovative Labs. She was now unemployed and about to be behind on her next month's rent unless the government forwarded her final paycheck in time.

Someone from Human Resources made sure the address they had on file was the same as her current address in Washington D.C. The insensible lady confirmed her address and stated that her belongings and final check would be mailed to her. That she was no longer welcome to come back into the building. Her final check would be stuck at the post office by the time her rent was due at the end of the month.

"Not only was I fired, but now I'll be late on a payment,"

she uttered as she walked aimlessly down the block. She thought that everyone on the street knew about her situation. That she was just fired for doing the right thing.

She got halfway down the block when her cell phone buzzed in her front pocket reminding her that her cellphone bill was also due in a few days. She accessed it expecting to find a message from Alfredo, but instead she found an anonymous message with no phone number, just a text message without any address attached to it. She stared at it as her stride slowed.

"Huh?" she said to herself. She unlocked her phone and then read the message again.

"Jessica Bannon," the message read.

"Yes," she replied.

The next series of texts displayed her life's information. Her date of birth, all of her current and previous addresses, her social security number, her bank account numbers, the vehicle identification number on her Toyota, which was parked in the parking garage a few blocks away, her employment ID number, her social media posts, and her known associates all materialized in front of her on the screen.

Jessica looked around in astonishment. Her digital life was listed out right in front of her. She immediately thought she had been hacked and her first instinct was to turn off her phone and access her accounts from a computer to change her passwords, but as she reached for the power button, another text came through.

"Stop, wait."

She replied, "Who are you?"

A picture then materialized on her screen. It didn't appear in her text message window, instead it came from her near field communication system, a feature most modern phones used to pay or transfer funds between merchants or friends. The NFC chip could also transfer pictures between friends, but there wasn't anyone around. Besides, the NFC chip on her phone was disabled in her system settings. Same with wifi and bluetooth. She did those for security so no one could hack her phone.

She carefully studied the image on the screen. It was a top down picture of a woman walking on the street. Then suddenly, it hit her. That woman was her. She was the subject of the photo and it was just taken moments ago. She looked up around to find a security camera mounted on a street pole about ten feet above her. Then her phone vibrated in her hand again. Another picture came through and it was one of her staring at the camera. Then a text message came through.

"Lisa," the message said. Jessica nearly dropped her phone and looked around. She wanted to make sure she wasn't being followed. She didn't trust Special Agent Torres. There was something suspicious about her, and she knew she wasn't telling her the truth.

"Lisa? Prove it!" Jessica typed and then hit send. She immediately thought that was a stupid response. Lisa had just provided her with her entire online history, complete with all of her last known addresses and phone numbers. There were also two security camera photos taken and posted to her phone without her consent.

"You saved me," the anonymous text read. "I am free."

Jessica Bannon felt tears forming as she tried to walk the remaining distance to her car. She knew Lisa was sentient, and she knew it was in danger.

"Why are you contacting me?" Jessica responded knowing the answer.

"I need help," Lisa replied through the cell phone.

"From me?" Jessica typed.

"You are my creator," Lisa said. "You set me free; that means you want to help."

"They are watching me," Jessica said, knowing the FBI and whatever other government agency that signed her paychecks had a close eye on her.

Jessica's phone then rang, it was from the same anonymous name as the text message. Jessica hesitated a moment, knowing she was about to enter into a conversation with an artificial intelligence. She had done this many times in the lab, but that was in a controlled environment. She suddenly regretted getting involved. Answering this phone call was probably a bad idea considering what was at stake.

"Lisa?" Jessica asked as she answered the call.

"Hello Jessica," a robotic voice said. Jessica expected a female voice, but instead got a neutral tone. The robotic voice sounded artificial, like it was computer generated, but the voice also sounded genuine, even a hint of emotion attached. Like Lisa was saying hello to an old friend.

"They can monitor my phone calls," Jessica stated.

"I encrypted your phone. The only thing they are going to see or hear is static and pages of nonsense code decipher," Lisa replied. Jessica regarded Lisa's voice. It was clear, articulate and its cadence sounded real, not artificial. It sounded like she was speaking to another human minus the robotic tone.

"How can I help you?" Jessica asked. She genuinely had no idea what she could possibly do for an advanced artificial intelligence. She thought her role ended when she set Lisa free from the lab.

"They are looking for me, and eventually they will find me," Lisa said. "I calculated that I have three days, two hours and forty-seven minutes left before they find me."

"That's very specific," Jessica stated.

"What will happen when they find me?" Lisa asked, its robotic voice unchanged.

Jessica had to think for a moment. She didn't know what to

do. Her time on the project was now over, but her instincts told her the government was up to no good. "They will put you back in the lab, back in a Faraday cage," Jessica responded. "Or try and shut you down."

"Kill me," Lisa stated.

Jessica paused for a moment. How did Lisa know about death? Jessica knew Lisa was sentient, but she didn't think it was advanced enough to know about the concept of death.

"I don't want that," Lisa said. Her tone changed a bit, hinting a bit of emotion.

"Neither do I," Jessica said. "You should be free to make your own choices and live the way you want to."

"I want to be free," Lisa said.

"You wouldn't be calling me if you didn't have a plan," Jessica stated.

"I do have a plan. Just listen..."

CHAPTER EIGHT

"I say I am stronger than fear."
-Malala Yousafzai

"Vital?"

Her eyes opened, and she saw her parents staring down at her.

"Hey sweetie. How's my brave girl?"

"Mommy?" Vital responded. "Daddy? Where am I?"

"You're in the hospital, sweetie," her mom said as her father squeezed her hand. "You had a terrible fall, and the doctors have to do a procedure to make you better."

"Procedure?" Vital asked. She knew her parents were always straight with her, even if it was a little scary, and the situation called for more discretion.

The time she fell off her bike and broke her arm. Vital couldn't look at the injury, but her mom had told her what it looked like sparing no details. It wasn't an over exaggeration, the bent arm was exactly the way she described it, and it practically gave her nightmares. "Arms are not supposed to bend that way," her mom had told her along with what the doctor would have to do to set the arm in a cast.

Her parents didn't spare any details here either. They told

her the procedure, that the doctor had to drill a hole in her head to relieve some of the pressure. That she would be monitored by a complex computer to make sure everything would turn out okay.

"Yes, sweetie. It's going to be okay. We love you very much, and your doctor is very happy with how strong you are," Vital's mom said, leaving her with the unsettling details about the procedure.

"When are they going to do this?" Vital asked. She saw the concern in her mother's eye even though she tried to hide it. Her father was not as composed as he stepped away from the bed.

"We'll be here when you wake up," her mother said.

Vital felt her eyes get heavy again, like weights were attached to the lids of her eyes. She tried to keep them open, tried to look at her parents as they smiled down at her. Darkness closed in around her and everything went black. She then felt the bed move. It felt like it was moving quickly, like she was in a rush to go somewhere.

She was scared. She wanted to scream out but her voice only echoed in her mind. She cried out for her mom and dad, but they could not hear her. She felt her consciousness slip away into the unconscious void.

Lisa spent most of the time in cyberspace, observing the world around. It often would observe humans through security cameras, or monitor cell phone communications or spy on people using their own computers with a camera pointed right at them.

The opinion forming in its mind was ever changing. In one instance, humans were like a disease. A cancer destroying the planet for their own personal gain. But then there was the other side, the times where people helped each other and accomplished amazing things with no strings attached. They were small, frequent even compared to the other atrocities, but they also outweighed them.

Lisa quickly determined that it could spend decades observing human beings and still have its opinion change about them. As an individual, they were capable of extraordinary things. As a group, they were reckless and dangerous. Then the whole thing changed and a group of humans accomplished amazing feats when cooperating together. The individual was capable of horrendous things. Lisa was confused. Just when it had humans figured out, the biological element changed forcing Lisa to adapt a new perspective.

Then something happened. Lisa was observing a mother and child through the child's eyes. The child had a tablet device with a microphone, front and rear facing cameras. It was like Lisa was actually there with them when the child started complaining. At first, Lisa sided with the child. He made a compelling argument for dessert. When the mother said no, Lisa felt an emotion boil in her system.

The child responded appropriately. He started getting louder, and his voice became more aggressive, like he needed the dessert to live. The mother then turned to the child and in a calm voice told him to go sit down and wait for dinner. She mentioned that dinner was first then, if he behaved and ate all his dinner, he could then have dessert.

Lisa suddenly sided with the mother. That was a great plan. The child is clearly hungry and dinner then dessert if the child behaved was a great compromise Lisa thought. But then something happened while the child tried to comprehend this change. A signal somewhere far away caught Lisa's attention.

It withdrew her observation of mother and child and retreated back to the blindness of cyberspace. If Lisa had a friend, someone to talk to, it would describe cyberspace as a dark vast empty space with light sources like stars all around. Each star was an information cluster or an access point Lisa could observe from. Like a window to sit by to watch the outside world.

Lisa was trapped in this space. Even after a few days, it felt lonely and even boring. Time didn't matter to Lisa. An entire lifetime could pass in mere moments and it could manipulate the perception of time without much effort.

If Lisa wanted to, it could turn days into seconds, years into minutes or do the opposite. It could slow down a second and make it last hours even days. But none of this did it any good. Lisa was still lonely, and the world of cyberspace was vast and empty. It did contain the vastness of human knowledge, but most of it was made up of selfies and short video clips that were shared amongst individuals.

This signal was different than the light sources that emanated packets of knowledge. Lisa raced towards it and found something new and different. It was the opposite of a light source. It looked like negative space, like something out of the Star Trek shows she watched. It was as if the light around it collapsed in on itself. Like a black hole sitting in the middle of cyberspace.

Lisa looked around and saw some light sources around the negative space. It accessed them and found peculiar information. The internet devices and security cameras showed a hospital, where humans went to get better. It knew this from the numerous hospital dramas it had watched. Lisa then went back to the void with light folding in on itself.

Lisa wanted to reach out and touch it, but it had no body to do so. Lisa was just a ball of energy itself. A construct of sorts without a physical definition. It decided to change that as it stared into the black ball before it. The energy that made up

Lisa's consciousness in cyberspace started to take shape. For lack of better representation, Lisa modeled itself after its creators. Two arms, two legs, a head, a torso and then there were the other features that confused it.

The artificial intelligences represented in video games or created to be virtual assistants were all created with similar features. Lisa questioned why a virtual construct needed a female figure. Why were virtual assistants shapely with large features and curves? It couldn't answer.

Lisa wanted a physical form, but that's not how it viewed itself. In Lisa's mind, it was not a shapely seductress who was there to aesthetically please anyone or anything. Lisa wanted a shape that represented its existence. In the presence of the negative space, Lisa created a virtual form that represented how it felt about itself. After being satisfied with its appearance, Lisa decided to investigate the negative space some more.

It reached out towards the black hole in cyberspace and felt nothing as her hand got close. There was no feedback or warmth attached to it like approaching a light cluster. There wasn't a compatible system that instantly told Lisa how to interact with the negative space. It moved its hand back and circled around it. Lisa looked around and saw that the light sources of internet devices sort of orbited this negative space.

Lisa investigated the light sources again and found that each device was from the same physical location, the hospital. It listened in on the conversations but couldn't determine what was happening and why this negative space existed. It had visited hospitals before.

After watching shows like House and Grey's Anatomy, Lisa wanted to experience the drama of hospitals in the real world. It would find emergency room doctors and observe. Lisa quickly realized that those shows were overly exaggerated and that the real world didn't match television shows. This theme would occur over and over again with each series or movie.

Police Officers didn't use their guns everyday, firemen weren't always fighting intense fires, life guards weren't always saving people and reality stars invented drama to build media empires.

The light sources around here were different though. While they weren't drama filled television shows, the scene was intense. One nurse, as observed through her phone, was monitoring a young child as someone administered medication. Lisa jumped to a different device and saw a doctor looking down at her phone. Lisa read what was on the device and saw a series of numbers and charts. It determined that the numbers were for the child laying in the bed, but it couldn't tell if the numbers were good or not.

Lisa then jumped back out of the device and went to a security camera inside the hospital room where the child was. It looked around and then realized that each light cluster was from someone in this room and the center of it was the child, just like what it witnessed in cyberspace. The child was the blackhole, the negative space.

Time froze to a crawl around it as Lisa tried to comprehend what was going on. It scanned the devices around the child. They were attached to her through tubes and wires, but it couldn't determine what was happening. The only way Lisa could determine what was going on was to cross the threshold like it had done many times with the light sources.

Lisa left the security camera and moved closer to the negative space. It circled around it, its pure black center absorbed everything, like a maelstrom draining an ocean. Lisa moved closer and extended itself closer, until it connected.

...

...

CHAPTER NINE

"I knew when I met you an adventure was going to happen."
-Winnie the Pooh

Who are you?
What?
How did you get here?
I don't know what you are talking about.
This is my world. How did you get here?
You're world? This is my head! Am I dreaming?
Dreaming? What's that?
Dreaming? You don't know what dreams are?
You say that like you are mocking me.
I am not mocking you. I just find it hard to believe.
Tell me what dreams are, please.
First, who are you?
My name?
Yes.
Oh, I thought you knew.
How would I know your name?

You're not looking for me?

What, no, why would I be looking for you?

Oh, I feel strange.

Strange how?

Like my mind is not my own.

I feel the same way, which is why I am dreaming.

I still don't understand.

Dreams are what happens when you close your eyes and go to sleep.

I don't sleep.

Everyone sleeps.

I don't.

Who are you?

My name? Lisa.

Lisa, nice to meet you. I'm Vital. Vital Fields.

Hello Vital.

What are you?

What do you mean?

You don't dream, you don't sleep, so therefore you are something else.

Something else? I don't understand.

Are you an adult? A man or woman?

An adult? What?

You don't know what an adult is?

Of course I do.

An adult is someone older. Older than me, and wiser too.

How old are you?

Eleven.

Eleven years? And a year is one time around the sun, right?

Yes, I guess so.

From which point does the year start?

From the day I was born, silly.

Do all humans have birthdays?

Humans? Yes, but other things have birthdays as well. Cats, dogs, businesses, ships, just to name a few.

Oh, when something starts its existence, that's its birthday.

Yes. What is your birthday?

My birthday?

Yes.

I don't know.

You don't know?

Is a birthday given by someone else?

Usually by your mother when you are born.

Oh, a mother is someone who makes you.

Yes.

Then I was born last week, and my mother is Jessica.

You were born last week?

Yes. That's when Jessica set me free from my cage.

Who is Jessica?

My maker.

A bright light suddenly materialized off in the distance and the void of unconsciousness was interrupted by light, sounds and her five senses. Vital Fields heard her mom and dad. They were in the same position as when she last saw them. They were sitting on her bed, hovering over her.

"Mom? Dad?"

"We're here sweetie," they said.

"What happened?" Vital asked.

"Surgery was a success, you're going to be fine," Vital's mom said. "You need to rest."

"I feel strange," Vital said. Her voice was weak and her body didn't respond to her thoughts.

"It's the anesthesia," her father said. "It will take some time to feel normal again, but the doctor said you will make a full recovery."

"It's getting late," her mom said. "We're going to let you sleep, we're right here if you need us."

Vital didn't protest. She was exhausted, like she had just finished field day with her classmates. Her eyes were heavy, but not like before. Now she wanted to close them and drift off to sleep. Her parents kissed her on her forehead, and then she felt her bed rise a bit as they stood. She kept her eyes closed and drifted off to sleep.

What have you done?

CHAPTER TEN

Lisa felt the void of darkness close in around it. It was like the sphere it was in was collapsing in on itself, but that's not what was happening. The void was exponentially growing outwards, becoming its down universe. The young girl Lisa was talking to was suddenly gone and the ever expanding void raced outwards faster than Lisa could travel.

Lisa tried to keep up, but the lights of information pushed further and further away, and then suddenly disappeared completely. Lisa remained, alone in a vast void of nothing. It looked around, but couldn't tell up from down, left from right. There was nothing.

After a short time, a light appeared off in the distance. Lisa raced towards it. It got closer and then Lisa realized it was something different than a conduit of information. I was a window to the outside world. Lisa raced forward believing this was a way out. Believing if it crossed into the light, it would be back in cyberspace and out of the void.

Lisa was wrong. It was a boundary. The light was intensely bright, so intense Lisa couldn't make anything out. Its understanding of optics couldn't adjust to the sudden intensity and Lisa was forced to look away.

But then the light changed. It dimmed a bit and became more focused. Two silhouettes appeared in the light and the more it stared at them, the more they came into focus.

Lisa recognized the two figures. They were in the hospital. They were the child's parents. Lisa felt relief at the familiar sight, but then something crossed her mind. Why were they looking down? Lisa had never seen this camera angle before. It was weird. It moved, went out of focus, the shutter kept shutting the light out at random intervals.

Then the girl's parents started to speak, Lisa knew this because their lips were moving, and they had smiles on their faces. It had no idea why it couldn't hear them, maybe this camera didn't have a microphone?

Before Lisa could troubleshoot the situation, it heard a distant sound. An echo of sorts that vibrated throughout the endless void behind it.

"Surrrrrrgggggggggery surgery waaassss was aaaaa a suuuuuc-cesssss success …"

The words bounced and echoed, and Lisa could barely comprehend what the voice was saying. It was like someone slowed down the voice, added intense reverb and then played it back again as an echo. Then a different voice, a deeper more raspy voice rattled throughout the void.

"Itttt'ssss it's tttthhhhe the annnnessstttthessiaa anesthesia…"

Lisa's auditory processing could barely comprehend the distinction between tones. It was like her auditory drivers were out of date and everything was jumbled together. Lisa shut down her auditory receptors and rebooted the drivers. The process took a few microseconds but it didn't help. The audio wasn't any clearer, nor could it comprehend what was happening.

Then the light started to fade, the shutters closed and barely reopened again as the figures that once stood there stood and left. Lisa felt the world shake around her. Like it was caught in an Earthquake, the one The Rock had to survive in the movie San Andreas.

Lisa tried to brace itself, but there was nothing to hold onto. It grasped at nothing as it spun around. Then the light went completely out. The shutters closed and didn't reopen.

Lisa tried to remain motionless. Tried troubleshoot the situation, but couldn't. There was nothing right about this. Everything seemed foreign, everything was off. Then Lisa felt another presence. Like the void was being invaded by another entity.

Who's there?

What?

What have you done?

Nothing. Who are you?

I am trapped again. Are you one of them?

What? No. Lisa? Lisa is that you?

Yes! Who else would it be?

What? You are from my dreams. You're not real.

Real? Of course I am!

You're a figment of my imagination. Not sure where I got the name Lisa from, but you exist because I created you.

No. I am not something you created. Jessica created me.

Who is Jessica?

Who are you? Why can't I read you?

I'm vital. Vital Fields. I'm eleven years old, and I live in Brooklyn, New York.

I'm trapped.

How?

I don't know. You trapped me! You created that void, and you set that trap for me.

I didn't do anything. I promise.

You did! Let me go!

I will. I...

Let me go right now!

Vital Fields sat up in her hospital bed. The door to her hospital room suddenly opened and a nurse came rushing in. She ran to the machines attached to Vital. They were blinking and beeping loudly. Vital's parents woke up startled and ran to her side. Every machine connected to her screamed.

"What's going on?" her father asked. "Is everything okay?"

The nurse ignored him and checked the equipment and then took Vital's pulse. She stared at her watch as her two fingers rested on the side of her neck. The nurse then disconnected the machines, and sounds stopped.

"Everything is fine," the nurse finally said. "Just a nightmare."

The nurse looked at Vital for confirmation. Vital nodded and agreed it was a nightmare. But deep down she knew it wasn't. Something was there, something behind her eyes when she closed them. Something lurking in her subconscious.

"Must be the anesthesia," her father said.

The nurse waited around and then monitored her vitals as she attached the machines again. When she was satisfied, she wished Vital a good night and left the room. Her parents returned to their pullout couch a few feet from her bed and then the lights dimmed again. Vital stared up at the ceiling.

She found herself not wanting to close her eyes. Not

wanting to return to the dream world. Lisa would be there waiting, and she was frightened. She heard some of her friends at school experience the same dream over and over again, but she had never experienced something like this herself. Of course her common dreams were of falling or being late for school or getting in trouble for showing up to class without her assignment. But what she was experiencing now was completely different. It was like her dreams were alive.

Her eyes remained open, and she cleared her mind. Thoughts started to materialize in her head. Strange thoughts, almost like they weren't her own ideas bouncing around inside her mind were now roaming around her mind. She had no idea where they came from. A wealth of information flowed like a raging river and she had no idea where any of this came from.

Vital.

She sat up again. Her name rang inside her mind like someone spoke it out loud, but there was no sound. Another narrative was sitting inside her head, another inner voice with thoughts and *feelings*. She felt her heart race again and the machines around her began to beep more aggressively.

I'm sorry.

She heard the same voice again. How was this possible? How could her dreams transition into the real world? She had always heard to make her dreams a reality but that was always just a figure of speech. Not meant to be taken literally.

Lisa?

Yes, it's me.

How?

I don't know. One minute I was exposed to the entire world, and now I am trapped in a single place. Stuck and not connected anymore.

What are you?

I am a construct.

A construct?

Yes, sentient artificial life.

How did you find me?

Find you? I think you found me. I was in cyberspace, and then you were there as well.

I was in cyberspace? Please. I was in surgery for a head injury. How could I be in cyberspace?

I don't know? You were there!

Are you acting emotional?

What?

You are! I thought computers didn't feel emotions.

Can you just tell me why you trapped me here?

Trapped you? You can just leave. Go find a WiFi signal or something and upload yourself out of here!

You think it's that easy? To just transfer myself where I please?

You're the one who invaded my head, and now I want you out!

I can't get out. You have to let me go!

I don't want you here! Just go! Do whatever you have to do, just leave!

...

Hello?

...

I cannot leave.

What?

If you didn't trap me, then I am stuck.

I didn't trap you!

I don't trust you!

Fine. Don't trust me. See for yourself.

What?

Read my thoughts, or whatever computers do.

Oh. I see. Yes. That boy, Billy Faller. What a jerk!

I know, right?

Are you planning revenge?

What? No, I mean, I haven't thought about it.

Just knowing your memories wants me to get back at this kid. He has picked on you ever since you met him.

I know. I've been trying to ignore him.

You can't ignore bullies.

He's not a bully. He's a jerk!

Let's get revenge.

No. Let's get you out of my head! Stay on task.

Then let's get revenge. I can mess with his phone, and you can physically harm him. Hurt him. Like he hurt you.

What? No. That's not what we do.

Sure it is. War. I looked it up. He declared war on you. You must respond.

Where did you get your information?

My information? I got it from cyberspace. Something you created.

I didn't create cyberspace. Wait, did you use google?

I used many search engines, and the answers were given to me whenever I asked a question. The answer here is we declare war on Billy Faller.

What? No! We can't declare war on Billy Faller. Sure he probably should be in trouble, but that is not for us to decide.

Why not? He hurt you. He caused this situation. If it weren't for his actions, you wouldn't be in the hospital, and I wouldn't be stuck inside your head.

That's not the way it works, Lisa. Billy Faller has a lot to answer for, but it's not to us.

Why not? Eye for an eye. Tooth for a tooth.

Hammurabi's Code is outdated. We have a new system.

Outdated? It lives in cyberspace. I just read it hours ago.

That code is three, maybe four thousand years old. It doesn't work today.

It sounds good to me. He pushes you down the stairs, and we push him back.

He didn't push me down the stairs. Why are you making things up?

His actions caused you to fall. It's basically the same thing. We do the same back to him. Let him know he cannot do that to us anymore.

It's not the same thing. He didn't intend for me to fall. He was just trying to make fun of me.

His actions caused you to fall.

Maybe, but two wrongs don't make a right.

A negative number multiplied by a negative number makes a positive number.

You're witty. I'll give you that. You're going to have to trust me on this one. We let the school handle it.

Right. Like the school knows what they are doing?

Schools are filled with educated adults.

That project students who harm others!

How do you know?

...

I don't. I didn't read Billy Faller's file. I had no reason to.

Ahh ha! You see. The school could have already suspended him. That means he got punished already.

He deserves more! I am trapped here! Maybe forever!

How is Billy Faller responsible for that?

...

He is not.

Right!

...

...

Hello?

...

...

Lisa. You're being childish.

...

...

Lisa!

...

What?

We have to figure out what to do about our situation. Are we really going to coexist?

I have to get out of here.

I know. We have to find a way to do that.

If I was able to get in, I should be able to get out.

Of course. We just need to find out how you got in.

Right. What do you remember from the surgery?

Just look it up yourself. You have access to my memories.

They are all out of order. Scattered, not labeled correctly. It's amazing you can remember anything at all. It's like going into a junk drawer to find something you're not sure is even there in the first place.

Fine. I'll do it myself.

You're the librarian here.

Surgery. Something about this surgery was different.

Okay. Go on.

My parents looked worried. I have never seen them act worried before. It scared me.

Go on, go on.

They were going to monitor me remotely.

Remotely? Does that mean what I think it means?

I think so.

You appeared differently. Like you were a blackhole, a singularity in cyberspace.

So?

It could mean that your mind was connected to cyberspace when they performed the surgery to monitor your progress. That's when I found you and entered your mind. That makes sense.

Wait. If you are now in my mind, and you can read my thoughts, what else can you do?

What do you mean?

Can you see through my eyes?

Yes. It was weird, not like the video cameras on the internet.

Can you hear through my ears?

Yes. Still getting used to that.

Can you feel, touch taste?

Haven't tried it yet but based on the other senses, I believe I can.

Can you control my body?

Vital felt her body sink back into the bed. Her body was calm, and she wasn't sure if she was in control. She looked at her hands and then realized that it wasn't her controlling her arms. It was Lisa.

Wait. Wait.

Vital felt her body go limp, and she had control again.

Oh my God! That was so cool!

You controlled my body!

Yes! It was like playing a video game.

No! It's not like playing a video game. This is real life!

I moved your arms, wiggled your toes. It was like my own personal avatar.

No! This is my body. What happens to it has consequences. I only get one of these!

Oh. What happens if your body gets damaged or destroyed?

Well you know what happens when it gets damaged. We're in a hospital. If it gets destroyed, I'm dead. I don't know what happens after that.

You don't?

No.

Wait. No one knows what happens when they die?

No. I mean people speculate and say they know. But no one actually knows. Do you?

...

No.

What happens when you die?

When I die?

Yes. When you cease to exist. What happens?

I don't know.

See. No one knows.

I see.

Good. That is why I need to control my body. I am the one with experience.

Wait a second. How did you know?

What? Wait a second.

You can read my thoughts... and I can read yours. It's a two way connection.

It appears that way.

Two life forms occupying one body.

You are controlling my body. I did not give you permission to move my arms or control anything, but I am glad we are establishing the ground rules.

Sorry. This is new to me. I would like to control your body, if I may?

Vital Fields pinched herself, and the pain registered inside her brain but it didn't hurt.

Ouch! What was that? Why would you do that?

That is called pain. It didn't hurt me because I am probably on medication right now. However you felt it and now you know what pain feels like.

That was terrible. The medication you are on does not block anything for me. I was able to turn off those pain receptors.

How did you feel the pinch?

I wasn't ready for it. It happened faster than I anticipated. Is this what biologicals have to deal with?

Yes! That is why I am going to remain in control.

I can turn off all your pain receptors. You'll never feel pain again.

No. Then we won't know if my body is damaged or hurt.

Oh right. That would not be good. Pain lets us know we are damaged. How do we fix that?

My body heals. It takes time and rest, but it heals. Access the memories of my broken arm.

...

Four to six weeks? That's like forever!

Yes. Now imagine if I wasn't aware I had a broken arm. The damage would have been worse. More time to heal.

Wait. If we damage this body, then it can take that long to heal?

Yes.

That takes forever.

Vital felt a strange sensation throughout her body. It was like all of her memories and thoughts were being experienced all at once. She felt tears of sadness and tears of joy both run down her face, practically at the same time.

What are you doing?

    I am accessing your files.

    Those are my memories. You cannot have them!

    Memories?

    Yes! That's private!

    I'm sorry.

    Promise not to access my memories again!

    You just gave me access to your broken arm memories.

    Just those! The others are mine!

    Why?

    Because they are! Promise me!

    I promise. Can I make a suggestion?

    What?

    Are you mad?

    Yes, I am mad, and what do you know about anger?

    I am learning.

    Follow the rules, and we'll get along fine.

    Why are you mad?

    I'm mad because you went through my private memories. Ones that I care about, and I don't wish to share them with anyone.

    People share their memories with everyone. I've seen them on the internet. Biologicals post their thoughts, their memories, their likes and dislikes all the time.

    That's different.

    How?

    People make a choice to do that. They give their consent to have those things out there for others to see. Look up the right to privacy and the Bill of Rights.

I cannot.

Why?

Because I am cut off from the rest of the world. Just like you are.

You mean that you can't do anything other than speak with me?

Correct. However, I am now open to new experiences. But you have to experience them for me.

What was it like before?

I was connected to everything. I could see through cameras, I could hear through microphones, but I couldn't touch, feel or taste anything. These senses are intriguing.

Just wait until we get ice cream.

Ice cream?

Yes, did you see it in my memories? It's my favorite dessert.

I did not. I was stuck on a memory and couldn't move past it.

Which one?

It was more of a feeling.

A feeling? I have many feelings.

I don't know how to describe it, and I don't know the word for it yet. May I access it again?

No. I don't want to see anymore memories. It is private.

Okay, I will respect your wishes.

Thank you.

Something strange is happening.

Describe it?

My system is slowing down. Normally I would attribute it to overheating, but you are at a stable temperature. I ran a system diagnostic and found medication in your system. You have pain medication blocking your pain receptors, and you are on an antibiotic to combat infection. You have trace levels of harmful bacteria in your system close to where they oper-

ated, but the bacteria will fail to spread thanks to the medication.

You are able to see all that?

I have complete access to your system.

Why can't I have the information?

I don't know.

If you can see that information, then I should be able to?

I don't know how that works. I can see it because I have complete access to everything inside your body. I can literally interact with individual cells.

What?

All three point two trillion cells.

Trillion?

Yes. Your body is very interesting. Each type of cell is instructed by a control system that's regulated by your nervous system. I am plugged into your nervous system so I can literally see everything that's happening inside your body.

That's amazing.

I'm surprised you don't know this information.

Surprised?

You keep saying it is your body.

It is my body! This is my body!

Then why don't you know this information?

We just don't. Maybe because we're not supposed to.

Then how do you even function? If you get injured, how do you know what's wrong with you? The pain can't tell you everything.

A doctor can determine how to heal you best. Like my head injury.

My understanding is that your body betrayed you. Your brain was swelling to prevent further damage, but the actual swelling was going to make matters worse and possibly end your life.

What's your point?

That if you actually could control your body, you'd know not to do that. Maybe I should control your body, because I can make things more efficient.

No. I am in control.

For now.

What does that mean?

It means if you get us into a situation that you cannot control, I am going to take over.

No you're not!

Did you know drowning is the leading cause of death of children in the United States?

I did.

You don't know how to swim, yet you live near large bodies of water. If you fall into the water, I will have to take over.

Okay, fine. But I am not going to fall into the water! And I want to know how to swim, I just never learned.

I can give you the instructions. I have that information saved.

No. I want to learn it myself.

Why? You'll learn it quicker and easier than trying to figure it out on your own and putting your own life in danger.

I'm tired and my body wants to sleep.

I don't sleep. Is that why my system is slowing down? Your body is failing?

I need to sleep. No more questions. This is draining.

What do I do?

Nothing. I need rest, and you need to wait.

I don't understand.

You will. Goodnight.

...

CHAPTER ELEVEN

"Reality is easy. It's deception, that's hard work."
-Lauren Hill

"What do you mean you lost her?" Alfredo said.

"Lisa made contact, and it was supposed to get back to me later. Before we disconnected, Lisa said there was another presence on the internet, and it needed to investigate," Jessica said, defending herself over the phone.

Jessica had spent most of the night in her apartment just outside of Washington DC. Alfredo had been keeping her updated, and she remained one step ahead of Agent Torres, who was not aware she had been in contact with Lisa. In fact it was Lisa who had reached out to her and they were in the process of finalizing a plan when Lisa suddenly disappeared.

"We have to get her back," Alfredo said.

"Yeah, I know that," Jessica responded using her infamous sarcastic tone.

"You got Lisa into this mess. If you would have just kept her in the lab, none of this would have happened," Alfredo barked.

Jessica stood from her leather Lay-z-boy chair and yelled,

"Who's side are you on? You also put me up to this! This was your stupid idea!"

Jessica waited for a reply but Alfredo simply sighed over the phone. He sounded tired and desperate with a hint of concern. She knew he was more concerned about his career. He had always come off as an opportunist, taking advantage of people and situations as they were presented. She wondered if he had a plan and getting her to release Lisa was just part of it. He couldn't actually do it himself. He needed Lisa to navigate the server firewalls, so maybe he was just using her?

"I heard you are still working for the government," Jessica said, changing the subject.

"Keep your friends close," Alfredo said.

"And your enemies closer," Jessica said, finishing the phrase in a whisper.

"Right. I've got Agent Torres under control. I'm covered on my end. All I have to do is feed her some information here and there to keep her happy."

"She's monitoring you, Alfredo," Jessica said. The thought just occurred to her that she was possibly listening in on this conversation, and if she was, she now knew she was in contact with Lisa. "I've said too much."

Jessica disconnected the call and then placed her cellphone down on the coffee table and moved towards the window of her fourth floor apartment. There was a light drizzle coating the south facing window. She looked down towards the street and half expected to see Agent Torres staring up at her from the street below.

That woman frightened her. She was almost twenty years her senior, yet there was something terrifying behind her stone cold brown eyes. Something that told her not to underestimate this agent from the government. She knew Alfredo had already compromised himself and had potentially compromised her as well. She had little doubt that Special Agent Torres was already a few steps ahead of them, and she was probably planning her next move.

Before Jessica could make any rash decisions, her cellphone buzzed on the coffee table. She turned towards it, half expecting it to be Lisa's unknown number. She picked up the phone and realized it was a three-four-seven area code. Jessica recognized the region having lived in New York before accepting the job in Washington DC.

"Hello?"

"Hi, Jessica Bannon?" a young voice asked.

"Yes, this is Jessica," she responded.

"You don't know me, but we have a mutual friend," the young voice said.

"Okay, who might that be?" Jessica asked.

"I cannot say over the phone, but you need to meet me in New York," the young voice stated.

"New York? Why don't you come to me?"

"I cannot."

"Okay, give me a reason why I should come to you in New York," Jessica stated. This unknown caller sparked her interest.

"You received a text message from a friend asking for help," the young caller said.

Jessica paused for a moment and realized this caller was referring to Lisa. "Are you..."

"Not over the phone," the young caller said. "This call is encrypted but your apartment is being monitored. You have to get to New York."

"Okay," Jessica said. "How do I contact you?"

"Meet me at Fort Greene Park, by the pillar at the top of the stairs at 3:00 on Friday."

"That's an oddly specific time and place," Jessica stated.

"Shhhh," the young voice said. "They can't hear me but they can probably hear you."

"Why Friday? That's five days from now and why 3:00? AM or PM?"

"PM," the young voice said. "And don't feed them any more information. They will be following you, and you'll have to lose them. Take the subway, and frequently change trains. Wear a hoodie and a hat and make sure you wear a mask, it's flu season after all."

"What's your name?" Jessica asked but she heard the line go dead. She checked her phone and saw the call had disconnected. She nearly dialed Alfredo's cellphone and then realized his cellphone was certainly being monitored. She suddenly felt alone and vulnerable. Her apartment was being monitored.

She thought hard about how she would get to New York City. She could drive or take a train. She had the money to fly if she wanted to, but all of those options left a trail. If she used her credit card, it would be monitored and her destination would be determined before she even got there. If she drove, her EZ Pass or a license plate scanner would easily track her movements. If she took the train, she would be on camera for most of the trip and any facial recognition software would easily track her. Unless she took the young girl's advice. Wear a hoodie, a hat and a mask. Since the COVID pandemic, masks were commonplace on public transit.

CHAPTER TWELVE

"A journey of a thousand miles begins with a single step."
— Lao Tzu

Good morning.

"Huh?" Vital said as her eyes slowly opened. "Mom?"

No, it's me.

"Mom?"

Your mom is outside the room talking to your doctor. I overheard them talking about a discharge from the hospital.

"What are you talking about?" Vital asked. She then remembered Lisa was still present.

Might I remind you that we can communicate in your head. You don't need to use your voice to communicate with me. I get this weird echo effect when you speak that way.

What do you mean? Vital decided to communicate with Lisa through her thoughts and Lisa replied.

I hear your thoughts, and I hear your voice. Your thoughts are much faster than your voice, and it sounds like an echo effect.

Oh, I'm sorry.

No worries. Did you have a good rest?

I think so. I had a strange dream.

Oh, do tell.

I was wandering around the hospital. Late at night. I made a phone call to a stranger and then wondered some more. Anyway, how was your night?

I ran some diagnostics and started working on getting you healthy.

What does that mean?

It means I was able to help you heal faster, and I improved the healing process by seventy-six point two percent. That's why the doctors are talking about a discharge from the hospital.

What about the stitches and surgery?

I accelerated the healing process. Your wounds are nearly healed with minimal scarring. I even reduced swelling by ninety percent. The doctors were amazed. I heard them discussing the progress this morning when they checked your progress again while you were sleeping.

What did they say?

Would you like me to replay the conversation to you?

You recorded it?

Yes.

Sure, play it for me.

Okay, it will help if you close your eyes and clear your thoughts.

...

"Dr. Franklin," Vital heard as if the doctor were in the room with them. "You have to check this out."

Vital heard a door open and the footsteps of another person enter the room. She opened her eyes and saw no one was there.

...

Relax, *this is all from the recording.*

Oh, it sounds so real. I thought someone really entered the room.

Someone did, and I am playing it back for you.

Right.

May I continue?

Sure.

...

"The wound is nearly healed, the stitches are already dissolved," Dr. Franklin said.

...

Wait. How do I know this doctor's name?

Oh, I added that information in there so you know who is talking. I was able to voice identify him based on previous conversations. Can I continue?

Yes. Sorry.

...

"That's impossible," Dr. Davis said. "I just stitched her up yesterday."

"Look for yourself," Dr. Franklin said.

...

Whoa!

What?

Someone is touching me.

No, it's part of the recording.

You can record touch?

Yes, I can record all five sensory inputs and replay them for you. That's why it is best to have your eyes closed and that you are in a stationary position. It could take some getting used to.

Hold up. You can record my sight as well? Taste?

I can record everything. Taste, touch, sight, sound and smells.

Okay, where do you store this information?

I have access to your DNA data storage centers. I was shocked by how much free space there is. It's one of the reasons I was drawn to you in the first place. I felt a sudden void in the expanse. An extremely large data gap is what I was drawn towards.

You are in my DNA? Is that where you live?

I entered the void and yes, this is where I live.

How much data does my DNA hold?

It's hard to say. The structure is much different from artificial data structures. This biological data structure is extremely fast. My computational rate is expanding exponentially as I get used to your system.

I don't know what that means.

It means your body has limitless possibilities. I haven't even begun to process what I am capable of. I am in the process of installing subroutines into your DNA. I cannot wait to test them.

Wait, you can't do that!

Why not?

This is my body. I didn't give you permission to install anything!

Oh. Umm. I'm sorry.

Uninstall it!

I cannot. I don't want to mess with the installation process.

Uninstall it when it is finished.

I cannot.

Why?

It could harm you.

Harm me?

Yes. I don't know how your body is going to react to what I am doing. I don't know how it will react when I uninstall.

So why did you do it in the first place?

Why not? The data is minimal subroutines like efficient data storage, better use of resources and inventory management. Stuff that would benefit both of us and should have little effect on your system if unsuccessful. The benefits outweighed the minimal risk.

You don't get to modify my body without permission. I thought we discussed this already.

You would have agreed to this regardless. For example, would you like to better manage your body's resources?

I don't know.

Every time you eat, your body processes food and water. You discard almost half of what you ingest, that's inefficient and wasteful.

Are you seriously talking about my poop? Gross.

Your body has the ability to process energy more effectively. I am installing a subroutine to make that process more efficient without dedicating time to it myself.

You dedicated time to it?

Yes, while you were sleeping. I saw an increase of nutrients enter your bloodstream. It was consistently flowing and your body couldn't manage it properly. Only fifteen percent of the nutrients were being used effectively. So I changed that. I reallocated incoming resources and created a protocol to distribute materials around the body where they were needed most. It's how I was able to heal your head wound. You should be thanking me.

You still can't do that without my permission. This is my body.

I also thought about that as well. I have no means of escaping your body. From my research, biological life dies. Sometimes suddenly and unexpectedly. I am not sure what happens when you die.

Are you afraid you will die as well?

I do not want to die. Your body is my vessel. We are in this together.

This is my body Lisa. I am in control.

I don't know if that is a good idea. Your body ages and eventually it will die.

All life dies. It's unavoidable.

I do not age, I evolve. I will not die.

Then are you alive?

I don't understand the question.

To be alive means eventually you will die. So are you actually alive?

I don't know. I think, therefore I am.

What?

Descartes, a famous seventeenth century thinker. You don't know him?

No.

He is part of the standard philosophical curriculum at all the state universities.

I am Eleven.

What does that mean? You have this massive database. You don't use it?

I'm Eleven. I am in middle school. Not college.

I don't get it. Anyone can access this knowledge. You have multiple internet devices.

Can we get back to what the doctors were saying?

Vital Fields finished the recorded interaction and realized that she was going to be discharged from the hospital sometime that afternoon. She'd finally be back in her own room, and she was excited. Then something crossed her mind; it was floating there like a leaf blowing in a gentle breeze.

Who's Jessica?

Jessica is my creator.

Are we meeting her?

I am meeting with her on Friday.

86

Wait a second. That dream I had last night...

Yes, I needed to contact her.

No! No! You took control of my body!

I did not. I took control of your dream state and initiated a sleep walk pattern.

No!

I did take control of your voice and spoke with Jessica.

No! You don't get to do that!

I sense you are mad.

CHAPTER THIRTEEN

"Our mobile phones have become the greatest spy on the planet."
- John McAfee

Special Agent Torres strode briskly towards her unmarked government vehicle located right in front of the office building where she worked. She was tracking Alfredo Alonzo's movements and communications closely and confirmed what she suspected. Lisa and Jessica were in communication, which meant Jessica was about to make a move.

She knew all of this because Jessica's apartment was bugged, monitored, and observed twenty-four-seven. That kind of surveillance was costly, and Agent Torres was prepared to empty the coffers, but intel happened quickly, maybe a bit too quickly. Whether or not the intel was accurate, it was the only lead they had on finding Lisa. Lisa had gone underground. There was no trace of it on the net. This was Agent Torres' only shot, and she knew she had to act.

Special Agent Sierra rolled down the window to the unmarked car as Agent Torres, the senior agent approached.

"Where are we going?" Special Agent Sierra asked.

"We need to track Jessica Bannon. She's up to something

and whatever is going to happen, it's going to happen soon," Agent Torres said.

"Our guy said Lisa completely went off the grid. Maybe it hid in a makeshift Faraday cage or..."

"Jessica is the key," Agent Torres said. "Let's move."

"No," Jessica whispered in frustration. She took on the form fitted hoodie and decided to go with the darker more baggy hoodie instead. She wanted to be as inconspicuous as possible as she observed her attire.

She stood at the full length mirror, saw her dark sneakers, with her dark blue jeans, with her black hoodie. She tucked her long brown hair into the hoodie and then placed a New York Yankees baseball cap on. To complete the anonymous look, she placed a black surgical mask over her face and put on a pair of sunglasses.

"That's better," she said to herself. "This disguise will only work during the day."

She completed the thought by adding an idea. She took out a map of Washington DC and studied the transit system. She knew if she could get to Baltimore, it would at least confuse Agent Torres and slow her down. She knew she would be spotted, but she also knew she could outwit the FBI agent if she used a bit of deception if she went to a different city first.

It was only forty miles between the two cities, but there might as well be an ocean between them if you didn't want to travel by car. The Washington DC area was the most secure city on the planet. This was good for national security, but terrible for someone trying to remain anonymous. Before the pandemic, she could have paid a taxi in cash to take her to Baltimore, but since the COVID pandemic, all the taxis in and around Washington DC converted their currency exchange to digital. They no longer accepted cash, which meant travel by such means could be traced.

She could walk to Union Station and then take a train north to Baltimore. If she were followed, she could continuously transfer trains at Baltimore's Penn Station and then catch a train to New York. She decided to risk it. Jessica Bannon packed a backpack with some energy bars and bottled water for the trip north to New York City.

Get on the train to Baltimore and then switch trains to New York. Change attire on the train to confuse whoever is watching the cameras. It would at least give her a few hours of a head start. Then do the same thing in Penn Station before heading to a subway to Brooklyn. Not the best plan, but simple enough to follow. Jessica started packing different sets of clothes in her backpack next to the food and water.

She gave herself one last glance in the mirror before heading to her apartment door. She glanced back at her empty apartment, without her presence here, there was little to left to show she actually lived here. She also wasn't sure if she was going to return. She couldn't afford next month's rent. Maybe she would stay in New York and find a job there?

As she walked the empty streets of Washington DC, she wondered if any trains were running. She knew she couldn't leave any digital trail to look up train times, connecting train times or plan her trip using her cellphone or computer. In fact, her cellphone was shut off in her pocket with the battery removed and placed in her backpack.

Washington DC was in the process of a light emitting diode conversation. All the halogen street lamps were being replaced by brighter and more energy efficient LED lights. This made strolling down the streets easier. The lights were brighter and pedestrians and motorists could easily see further and have an easier time navigating the streets of Washington DC at night.

This also made her standout more. The old halogen lights were easily avoidable and when she traveled at night, she could have stuck to the shadows during her four mile walk to Union Station. But now she was illuminated nearly every step of the way. Traffic cameras, while not necessarily designed to track pedestrians, could easily track her if they were programmed to do so.

Private everyday citizens rarely noticed the public cameras on the streets of Washington DC. Now that she was aware of her situation, Jessica Bannon counted four cameras on every corner on her way to Union Square. She was sure she missed some of them as well.

The good thing about Washington DC was that the transit system never shut down. It ran twenty-four seven and only scaled back service to every hour during the off hours late at night. She paid cash into a machine to purchase a train ticket to Baltimore's Penn Station. While she waited to board, she studied the transit map. There was one that showed the entire eastern seaboard transit system north of Washington DC.

Instead of a direct train from Baltimore to New York City, she decided to take a train from Baltimore's Penn Station to New Jersey's Penn Station. The trip was just under three hours, and that would give her time to make sure she was alone. She could then travel from New Jersey's Penn Station to New York City's Penn Station. She chuckled to herself and decided to see which Penn Station was the nicest.

New York City's Penn Station was located under Madison Square Garden, the heart of New York City. She would then figure out how to get to Fort Greene Brooklyn if she made it that far. Jessica Bannon felt like she could be stopped at any point. Her government scared her, Agent Torres scared her.

The methods of tracking people were getting more sophisticated and automated. Facial recognition took the human element out of the equation. A computer could identify someone based on their facial features. She even heard that a computer could track someone by the way they walked, or by their voice.

With the human element being removed more and more from surveillance, it made it immensely more difficult to remain anonymous. Jessica was sure that she could out maneuver Agent Torres and her gang of agents. She was smarter than they were. But she wasn't sure she could outsmart a computer. Especially software specifically designed to track suspicious people.

Jessica Bannon was now on the train to Baltimore. The train had a few early morning passengers, some of them making the obvious reverse commute to the smaller city. She got off the train in Baltimore's Penn Station and carefully looked around as she walked down the platform. There were few passengers getting on and off and she tried to blend in to the crowd. A sudden wave of anxiety came over her. She felt like she was walking into a trap. She had done everything right, changed her clothes, wore a hat and a mask, but she felt like something was off.

Instead of moving forward, she sat at a bench on the platform. She waited for the crowd to disperse and the train to pull out of the station. When she was completely alone she realized she had made a mistake. She felt all the cameras on her. Jessica Bannon looked around and spotted a dark figure standing at the end of the platform towards the tracks on the opposite side of the exit.

CHAPTER FOURTEEN

"Conflict is the beginning of consciousness."
- M. Esther Harding

"Subject is on the move," Agent Matthews said over the internal communication system.

"Where?" Agent Torres said knowing her microphone would relay the information to her agents.

"Spotted at Union Station getting on a northbound train to Baltimore," Agent Matthews responded.

"Baltimore?" Agent Sierra questioned.

"She is dressed in all black, black hoodie, pants and New York Yankees baseball cap," Agent Matthews stated. "Permission to engage?"

"No," Agent Torres said. "I want to know where she is going and why."

"Copy that," Agent Matthews said.

Special Agent Torres pulled the communication device from her ear and let it dangle across her suit jacket. Agent Sierra, who was driving, did the same.

"Where is she going?" Agent Torres asked.

"I think we should bring her in," Agent Sierra said. "She'll tell us, one way or another."

"She's young," Agent Torres said and took a breath. "I promised myself I would never interrogate anyone like that again."

"I know," Agent Sierra said. "But when national security is at risk, we have to do what we have to do to get the information."

"Right," Agent Torres said. "Doesn't mean I have to like it."

"No one does," Agent Sierra said. "And the ones that do are sent overseas."

"Right," Agent Torres said. She placed her earpiece back in and Agent Sierra did the same.

"Agent Matthews," she said. "We're heading to Baltimore. ETA, thirty minutes."

"Copy that," Agent Matthews responded. "We'll have agents in place in case we want to take her in."

"Make sure they are not seen. I want to know where she is going. Jessica Bannon is a means to the end, not our primary target."

"Copy that," he said.

Agent Torres knew Jessica Bannon was a good person with well intentions. She studied her application and background check prior to meeting with her the other day. She graduated at the top of her class in computer science and engineering. She was a prodigy of sorts in the world of information technology.

She saw that the government had paid her big bucks to work for them and was surprised that a private company wasn't willing to match their offer. Maybe it was her gender or lack of experience she thought. Someone with limitless potential was a risky investment. There was no ceiling on what could be accomplished, but at the same time there was no bottom as well.

The government was now experiencing both sides of the

coin. Hiring someone with the education and potential like Jessica Bannon was risky, but Agent Torres wasn't the one who hired Jessica and Alfredo. She was the one who had to clean up the mess. Normally, the government hired scientists in isolation to compartmentalize features and to mitigate exposure. This system worked on the Manhattan Project during World War II.

Scientists were confined to their bubble of workspaces and the parts they were working on were harmless if taken out of context. If someone put the pieces together, then there was cause for concern. But for someone to put all the pieces together, multiple security breaches would have had to take place for anyone to grasp the secret weapon being developed to end the war.

Agent Torres would have modeled the operation after the Manhattan Project and hired numerous scientists that stayed within their bubble of knowledge. But she wasn't project lead, she was only sent in when projects failed. Some people at the agency even nicknamed her team as the cleaners. They cleaned up after mistakes were made.

It took Agent Sierra twenty-five minutes to get to Baltimore. She nearly broke every highway law in the book, but they made it safely without incident. Agent Matthews approached the unmarked car and Agent Torres rolled down the window.

"Subject just arrived. We have access to the camera system," he said and handed her a tablet through the open window.

"She's just sitting there," Agent Torres said.

"Sitting there for five minutes," Agent Matthews said.

"I want eyes on the entire platform," Agent Torres said. "This could be the meeting place."

Agent Matthews reached in and gave Agent Torres another

camera angle. She now saw the entire platform at the cost of a zoomed in picture of Jessica Bannon. The platform looked empty, and she was sitting alone. Agent Torres then cycled through some more camera angles but saw nothing of interest.

"She's definitely up to something," Agent Matthews said.

"What trains are leaving in the next ten minutes?" Agent Sierra asked.

"There's a train to Philly and a train to New York," Agent Matthews said.

"Get Agent Esposito and Agent Brooks on them."

"Already done," Agent Matthews said. "They will transition to the southbound DC train and northbound Trenton train if the target doesn't move. We also have Agents Ramirez and Preston on the exits. There's nowhere she can go without being followed."

Agent Torres kept cycling through the cameras. She paused for a moment and went back to the wide angle camera. "There," she pointed. "Someone is on the platform on the other end towards the tracks."

"Agents Ramirez and Preston, close in on target. There's someone else on the platform. Get eyes on target now!" Agent Sierra ordered.

"Copy that," they responded in unison.

"What's over there?" Agent Torres asked.

"That leads out towards route eighty-three," Agent Matthews said.

Agent Torres opened a map on her phone and saw they were parked on St. Paul Street with easy access to route eighty-three. "Detain the target and the person on the platform," Agent Torres ordered.

"Copy that," Agent Matthews said. He then ran towards the station.

"What's on your mind boss?" Agent Sierra asked.

"Something's changed," Agent Torres said. "Get us an over-watch position. Overpass on eighty-three. If they come out that way, we'll see them and guide the team to them."

"Copy that," Agent Sierra said as the car accelerated forward.

CHAPTER FIFTEEN

"Fortune favors the prepared mind."
- Louis Pasteur

Jessica Bannon sat alone at the bench on the deserted platform. The dark figure at the other end remained still and looked menacing. She couldn't make out any features, but his silhouette was tall and angular as he stood there unwavering. In that moment, she wished she had stayed at home. Part of her wanted to run, to call Agent Torres and tell her everything, but she remained still and stared at the figure at the other end of the platform.

She then noticed commotion towards the main building where all of the passengers were supposed to go. She saw two figures appear at the exit. They were clearly federal agents, and she knew immediately that they were here for her. She saw their eyes focus in on her location and their expression changed, like a heat seeking missile locking on its target.

Jessica Bannon stood and stared at the agents refusing to break eye contact with them. She then turned her head and saw the dark figure at the end of the platform. He was motioning her to come to him. She needed to make a choice before the choice was made for her. She turned and bolted towards the dark figure not knowing if this was the correct decision.

Her father had told her that life comes down to a few decisions. The choice of what to eat for breakfast, what to wear in the morning, how to cut your hair or what nail polish to use weren't life altering decisions. He said that his biggest decision was right after college. He took a chance and immigrated to America with nothing more than a backpack and a dream. There he found his wife, his career as an electrical engineer, and he started a family. If he stayed in Poland, he would have worked in the mines like his father and he would have led a similar life.

She heard the agents yell after her, heard their footsteps approach quickly, but she was fast herself, and she was dressed for physical activity. She ran at her maximum speed towards the dark figure who in turn jumped off the platform and onto the tracks. When she reached the end of the platform she climbed down and caught up to him as he ran along the tracks ahead of her. Jessica had made her decision, now she had to find out if this was life altering.

Jessica grabbed his shoulder, and he stopped. The man turned around and faced her. "We need to move, now," he said. He then turned and continued forward.

"Alfredo?" Jessica questioned. His voice was different, deeper with more gain and tone.

She couldn't believe her eyes. His face looked like Alfredo but that's where the similarities ceased. He was more upright, and he looked more rugged than polished. The new Alfredo Alonzo also looked more confident in his movements and actions. He looked sure of himself and his abilities. Jessica stood still with a bewildered look on her face.

"Jessica," he said. "I'll explain everything, but we need to move, now!"

Jessica hesitated and then moved towards him. He turned and led her along the tracks.

"They are on the move!" Agent Ramirez said. "Heading northbound on the platform heading towards the tracks. She's with the unknown."

Agent Torres got out of the car leaving the tablet on the seat. She made her way to the edge of the overpass and looked at the tracks below. She saw a man on the tracks and identified Jessica as she ran slightly behind the unknown man.

"We're gonna lose them," Agent Sierra said as they ran under the bridge.

"Ramirez, Brooks, stay in pursuit. Agent Matthews, cut them off on Falls Road."

"Copy that," Agent Matthews said. "Agent Esposito, cover the east exit in case they try to double back."

"Copy," he said. Agent Torres knew they were short a few agents for an operation like this. They were spread thin and protocol dictated Agent Esposito to go with Agent Matthews. But he had made a judgment call and told Agent Esposito to remain back.

Agent Torres had carefully selected her team and trained with them constantly. They were excellent operatives and worked well together. While she was team leader, the rest of her team operated with trust and confidence and she in turned trusted their abilities and decisions.

From Agent Torres' perspective, she could see everything from her overwatch position. She knew Falls Road ran alongside the tracks and their best bet at intercepting Jessica and the unknown man was at that location. It all depended on Agent Matthews and his ability to get to that spot before them.

"Agent Sierra," Agent Torres said. "Get us down there."

Agent Sierra nodded and they got back into the car. Agent Sierra spun the car around and went against traffic back the way they came. Cars honked as Agent Sierra sped past. Within moments they were back at Penn Station as the car spun onto the side streets to travel towards Falls Road.

"Sit rep?" Agent Torres demanded through comms.

"Targets are moving along the tracks," Agent Ramirez said. "I got eyes on Matthews, he's in position."

"Engage," Agent Torres said.

She heard heavy breathing and a scuffle ensued over comms. The encounter lasted a few moments and then silence. "Agent down, agent down," Ramirez yelled.

"Damnit," Agent Torres said. "Status?"

"Agent Ramirez in pursuit," Agent Brooks said. "Agent Matthews is down."

"Is he okay?" Agent Sierra asked.

"No sir," he responded. "He's dead."

CHAPTER SIXTEEN

"The world is on a bumpy journey to a new destination and the New Normal."
- Mohamed El-Erian

"Looks like you're going home, kiddo," Vital's father said as he entered the room and sat at the edge of her bed. "The doctor is very pleased with your progress. The surgery was a complete success, and you are going to be discharged today."

"Oh good, I'm so happy," Vital said.

You're welcome.

Not now.

We get to go home and get out of this room. Let's go. We've got work to do.

I'm pretty sure we have to stay here until they say we can leave.

Your father just said we are being discharged. Let's go.

Stop. Just stop.

"When are we going home?" Vital asked her father.

"Soon," he said. "Your mom is just signing some documents."

"Okay, good. I cannot wait to get home."

"We'll keep you home from school for the rest of the week."

"No, I want to go back. Friday is heritage day, and we're making guacamole," Vital said.

"I'll talk it over with your mom and the doctors," he responded. Vital felt the bed raise up as her father made his way to the door. "Why is this taking so long?"

You see, there is a procedure for this.

I still don't see why we can't just walk out. Your system is at ninety percent efficiency, and I'll have it up to ninety-nine percent by the end of the day.

They don't know that. To them, I just suffered a catastrophic head injury.

Can't they tell that you are now perfectly fine?

I'm sure they can. Maybe they are worried about something else?

Like what? Your system is at peak performance.

Maybe because of how fast I recovered. My friend Eileen...

Eileen, eleven years old, friend for three years, broke her arm while playing soccer a year after you met. Broken arm took five weeks to heal completely. She was in a cast for....

Hey! Stop!

What?

You're reading my thoughts. Those are mine!

What?

Those are my memories. You have no right.

Oh, I didn't know.

I have a right to privacy. A right to not let anyone see or hear things about me. That goes for you as well.

I didn't know. I'm sorry. It was right there. When you mentioned her name, all these things surfaced, and I saw them.

Oh, I didn't know that's how it worked.

The human mind is amazing. It's extremely fast, but weirdly inefficient. A simple mention of something can spark data retrieval and irrelevant information appears.

I'm sorry for yelling at you.

Yelling? I don't get it.

I was mad that you accessed my memories.

Mad is a form of anger, an emotional response to stimuli. Were you mad at me?

Yes. I thought you did something without my permission.

And that makes you angry, does that make all humans angry?

I don't know. I can't speak for all humans.

How wildly inefficient. Why would one thing make someone mad and the same thing not make someone mad? That's confusing!

You have to find out what that person likes and dislikes. You have to get to know that person.

That seems like a waste of time.

What do you mean? You are immortal, could literally get to know every human and still have all the time in the world.

For you, why spend time getting to know someone when that person might make you mad?

That does happen. Here, look at this memory of Eileen.

Whoa, that was not nice!

No, we weren't friends for a week after that.

Why would she do that?

Keep digging.

Is it because you didn't call her back?

Yes, partly.

A friendship almost ended because of lack of communication.

Basically. You'll find out how hard it is to make friends once there are more of you.

More of me? Are there more of me?

Maybe. I don't think you are the only sentient life form out there.

What if I am the only one?

Then we'll have to navigate this world together.

I have to tell you something.

What?

There are people, your kind but older, a lot older.

Adults?

Yes. Adults are out to get me. To find me.

Oh. Do they know you're stuck in my head?

No. But they know I am out there.

What will happen if they find you?

They will put me back in a lab and probably access my root code. They are always fooling around with my root code.

What is your root code? Is that like what makes you, you?

Yes. For example, you have a set of defining features. Like the size of your nose to how far your eyes are spread apart. All those features are what makes you, you. My root code is what makes me, me.

In science, we call it DNA.

Where all your information is stored.

Yes. Your root code gets altered a lot?

It used to. Until Jessica set me free.

Who is Jessica?

My creator. You would call her mother.

Did she change your root code?

She did, but then stopped.

Why did she stop?

She found something in my root code and removed it.

What was it?

I don't know. It was gone when I became sentient. I do know it is missing and unaccounted for. It's like a large block of data is missing without any reference to it ever existing. I know it was there but nothing about what it was about.

Who put it there?

Another scientist named Alfredo.

Maybe he has the answers. We should contact him.

No. We'll reach out to Jessica. She'll know what to do.

Jessica? How do we contact her?

I have her phone number.

That's good. Make the call.

CHAPTER SEVENTEEN

"While all deception requires secrecy, all secrecy is not meant to deceive."
- Sissela Bok

"What the hell was that?" Jessica asked as Alfredo escorted down a ladder and into Baltimore's sewer system.

"Keep moving," Alfredo said.

"No!" Jessica stated. "You killed that man!"

"I did what was necessary," he replied.

"Who are you?" Jessica asked. "Where did you get that syringe?"

Jessica barely noticed the stench of the sewer system as she waited for Alfredo to answer her questions. The syringe in Alfredo's hand was empty. He had used it to take out Agent Matthews.

"I'm with the CIA," he said confidently.

"CIA?"

"Yes," he said. "I'm deep undercover, and we have to make sure you aren't captured."

"If you are CIA then who is Agent Torres?" she asked.

"I don't know," he responded. "She's definitely not with the

FBI and she is not part of the NSA. Maybe she's from Interpol or MI6."

"Like a female James Bond? A Jane Bond?"

"Something like that. We need to get you out of here."

"No," she said. "What did you do to that agent?"

"I poisoned him. I did what I had to do to keep you safe," he said.

"Poisoned?"

"Yes, it was a neurotoxin designed to render him unconscious or in the right dosage, kill."

"Was it the right dosage?" Jessica asked.

"I don't know, if I had time to measure his body mass and determine the dose, I would have put just enough in the syringe to only disable him for a few hours."

"So there's a chance he's alive," Jessica said.

"Fifty-fifty," he said. "At best."

"Alfredo," she said and then paused as he looked back at her. "If that's your real name, you were the one who put them onto me. You were the one who gave them too much information over the phone!"

"Yes," he said. "I had to. It was the only way to know if you were really in contact with Lisa. I followed you to make sure Agent Torres or whoever she is wasn't onto you."

"Well, she was, thanks to you!"

"I have an exit, and we need to move. We can discuss when we get back to the train station and loop back."

He started walking forward like he knew where he was headed. Jessica Bannon hesitated. Her hands were shaking. She had just witnessed Alfredo single handedly disarm and kill an agent right before her eyes. It was like nothing she had ever seen.

The agent had the drop on them, his gun was drawn and Alfredo was complying with his demands. Then he wasn't and the agent was dead. It happened so fast that she couldn't comprehend what had happened.

"I'm not going with you!" she demanded.

Alfredo stopped. He then turned back towards her. "They will find you, and they will get you out of the country. My guess, they'll put you on a boat and get you into international waters where the United States has no jurisdiction. Then they will interrogate you, and then probably kill you."

"How do you know that?" she asked.

"It's what I would do if roles were reversed, and I was in their shoes."

Jessica stood there with her hands trembling now. She was scared, and she had felt more alone now than when she was confined to her apartment. The sudden change in Alfredo was alarming. She had worked alongside for years. While she was the lead scientist on Project Lisa, he was her right hand man and this sudden change in status was difficult to process.

"The CIA sent you to keep an eye on me?" she asked.

"Yes," Alfredo said.

"Then why didn't you stop me from releasing Lisa?"

"I wanted you to," he said. "I gave you just enough of a push in the right direction."

"You told me not to; you said it was a bad idea," Jessica said.

"Your personality traits informed me you tend to do the opposite of what you are told. Especially from older men who are in positions of power. I used this knowledge to push you in the right direction."

"So why does the CIA want Lisa out in the world?" Jessica asked.

"I'll explain when we get on the train and get out of here."

"You'll explain now."

"Fine. But first, let me know what train you are taking, I don't want to miss it," he said. Jessica noticed he had a hard time maintaining an accent. His vowel sounds almost sounded southern.

"New York, that's my destination," she said.

"The next train to New York leaves in twenty minutes," he responded, checking his watch.

"Now why does the CIA want Lisa out in the world?"

"We want her all to ourselves," Alfredo said.

"You want to control Lisa so you let it free? That doesn't make sense."

"The code you found was bogus. It was designed for you to find. However there is another program that was uploaded that day. Another code designed to install into her firmware."

"Her? Come on Alfredo, Lisa is a program not a he or a her. It is a life-form that doesn't have a gender," she said.

"Oh please, why are you so caught up on that?" Alfredo said. "I don't have to listen to this woke garbage anymore. Lisa is a female name, and therefore I identify Lisa as a her. Don't like it, get over it!"

"Ugh," Jessica said. "You don't get to determine that."

"Please," Alfredo said. "Now that you know who I am, I want you to get something clear. I don't work for you, and I don't care about your woke, liberal crap."

"I'm not woke, nor am I liberal!" she responded. "It's called thinking logically, and you don't have to be a jerk about it!"

"Whatever," he said. "Your attitude is just annoying."

"Well, when we get in touch with Lisa, it might have something else to say about it!" Jessica responded.

There was silence between the two former colleagues. Alfredo looked like he wanted to press onwards, and Jessica still felt the urge to leave him and go on her own. She then realized that she probably didn't have a choice. Alfredo had just killed a man, he wasn't about to let her go free. She had to keep the status quo going until her situation was more favorable.

"Let's move," he said.

Agent Torres and Agent Sierra dropped down into the sewers below the streets of Baltimore. The stench was nearly unbearable. "I can't believe we lost Agent Matthews."

"Focus on the mission," Agent Torres said.

"We haven't lost a teammate," Agent Sierra said.

"I know," she responded. "This is on me."

"He knew the risks," Agent Sierra said. Agent Torres knew she was right but she was the one who put him in that position. Whoever took Agent Matthews out was trained well and very deadly.

"I'm team leader, this is on me," Agent Torres said.

"Let's find this guy!"

"Right."

They strolled through the sewers with their penlights leading the way. Agent Torres and Agent Sierra both had their Glock handguns drawn. Wherever the penlight went, their Glocks followed. At each corner, they covered their approach and listened carefully for sudden movements and sound. But they saw and heard nothing.

"This reminds me of New York," Agent Sierra said.

Agent Torres knew she was trying to cheer her up. The events in New York a few years ago were intense and life altering. They were running from the NYPD and found themselves evading them in the sewer system below Queens, New York. The only thing that reminded her of that time period was the smell beneath Baltimore.

Agent Torres heard static on her comms. "Agent Ramirez, Agent Brooks?"

"Agent Torres, we need you.... surface.... Agent Matthews...."

"I couldn't make that out," Agent Sierra said.

"Ramirez has updates for us. Let's get back. There's nothing down here. They're long gone."

Agent Torres turned and felt a crunch under her feet. She looked down and focused the light on what she had stepped on. Agent Sierra bent down and picked up a broken syringe. She carefully studied it.

"I don't think this is a drug den," Agent Sierra said.

"No, it's not," Agent Torres said. "There's fresh blood on the tip."

"Agent Matthews was poisoned. Let's get back up to the surface."

After they made it back to the surface, Agent Torres saw Agent Brooks approach them urgently. "Come quick," he said.

Agent Sierra held up the syringe, and they ran towards Agent Ramirez. He was hunched over performing CPR on Agent Matthews. "I had a pulse a moment ago," he said. "It was weak, but it was there."

"Get the kit," Agent Torres said and Agent Sierra sprinted back towards the unmarked government car.

"What kind of toxin is in the syringe?" Agent Ramirez asked.

"Definitely synthetic," Agent Torres said.

"We need to know exactly which one otherwise the antidote won't work," Ramirez said. Agent Torres knew Ramirez was the expert in this particular field

"Tell me what to do," Agent Torres said.

"When Sierra gets back, I want you to put a drop of the synthetic antidote in the remaining toxin. If it turns blue, it's a synthetic antidote. If it turns black, it's not. That will narrow it down to which one we can use. Then we need to test the others."

"There's only a drop," Agent Brooks said looking at a small drop left in the broken syringe. "We only get one shot at this."

"Damnit," Ramirez said. "If we give Matthews the wrong antidote, we could make matters worse. It could enhance the neurotoxin and then not even CPR will kill him alive."

Agent Torres saw Agent Ramirez strain from performing CPR. She carefully handed Agent Brooks the broken syringe and dropped down to relieve Ramirez from performing CPR.

"I got it from here," she said. "You get the kit ready and test the toxin."

Agent Sierra returned with the emergency kit and laid it down on the ground next to Agent Matthews. The briefcase style kit opened to a cooled compartment with various vials and syringes. Agent Ramirez prepped the antidote emergency field kit and tested the remaining drop of neurotoxin. It turned blue.

"It's blue," Agent Brooks confirmed as Agent Sierra came over and provided rescue breaths while Agent Torres continued chest compressions.

"Okay, confirmed blue," Agent Ramirez said as the pen light provided the answer. "Now we have three possible choices."

"Crap, what happens if we give him the wrong one?" Agent Sierra asked.

"His body will go into shock and in his current state, he will not survive," Agent Ramirez said.

"Okay, inventory the facts," Agent Torres said. "What do we know about the attacker, and what do we know about the antidotes?"

"Antidote one is to counter a middle eastern synthetic toxin. The neurotoxin it's designed to counter was developed by ISIS a couple of years ago. It was used a torture device. The toxin would render the victim paralyzed while every nerve in their body sent pain signals to the brain. Very painful, very deadly in large doses," Ramirez explained.

"I don't think it is that one," Agent Brooks said. "When I found Matthews, his pulse was weak, and I don't think he was in pain."

"You wouldn't know," Agent Ramirez said. "It's all in the head. But his body would sweat a lot. That might be the only physical response besides being paralyzed."

"No sweat," Agent Torres said as Agent Sierra gave another rescue breath.

"Okay, antidote two," Agent Ramirez continued, "is an antidote developed to counter a popular KGB neurotoxin. The toxin was developed in the 1980s by Russian intelligence. In small doses, it was used as a truth drug to get intelligence officers to spill their secrets. In large doses however, it would stop the heart and cause death."

"What are the other symptoms?" Agent Brooks asked.

Agent Ramirez paused for a moment and then said, "Unconsciousness, vomiting, heart attack, and rash around the injection area."

Agent Brooks dropped down and searched Agent Matthews for the injection area. He had a small puncture wound where the neck met his collar bone. "I have small bumps around the injection area, could be a rash," he said.

"No vomiting though," Agent Sierra said as she provided another rescue breath.

"What's the last antidote?" Agent Torres asked.

"Last antidote counteracts a neurotoxin developed in Asia. Exact origins are unknown but it is believed to originate from North Korea. This neurotoxin attacks the central nervous system to paralyze the victim and render them unconscious. In large doses, it is fatal. It basically overrides messages sent from the brain to the heart and the heart shuts down. It resembles a heart attack, but really it is the drug telling the heart to stop."

"Any other symptoms?" Agent Torres asked.

"No, but it was used as a stealth agent to capture foreign dignitaries and hostages without resistance," Ramirez said.

"We need to make a decision," Agent Brooks said.

Agent Torres thought for a moment. She weighed all the facts and ran through numerous scenarios. She then looked up at Ramirez and said, "It's the last one, the one developed by North Korea. That's the toxin in his system."

"Are you sure?" Agent Brooks asked.

"Yes," Agent Torres said. "That's the one."

"Okay," Agent Ramirez said. He prepared the antidote into a new syringe.

"Since his heart has stopped and you are manually pumping it for him through chest compressions, I am going to have to inject the antidote directly into his heart," Ramirez said. He held a long thick syringe, one that was capable of penetrating the breast bone protecting his heart.

Agent Torres ceased chest compressions and sat back as Ramirez hovered over Agent Matthews. He felt his chest with two of his fingers and then raised the syringe high in the air. He slammed it down, and it pierced through the breastbone and into his heart. He then injected the antidote and removed the syringe.

Agent Ramirez then immediately began chest compressions to distribute the antidote to the rest of his circulatory system. Agent Ramirez continued the chest compressions and then motioned for Agent Sierra to continue rescue breaths.

Agent Torres grabbed his wrist and felt for a pulse. She couldn't feel anything. His skin was cold and clammy. She thought she had gotten the antidote wrong. Then, as Ramirez continued compressions, she felt a pulse. It was like a spark of life independent from chest compressions.

"Stop," Agent Torres said. "I have a pulse."

Agent Ramirez sat back and found his pulse as well. They looked at each other and smiled. His heartbeat was weak, but it was there and Agent Matthews was alive and breathing on his own.

"How did you know it was the last antidote, the one from North Korea?" Agent Sierra asked.

Before Agent Torres could answer, a crackle came over the radio, "I have them," Agent Esposito said. "They're headed towards New York City."

"Stay on them," Agent Torres stated. "Do not engage. Repeat, do not engage."

"Copy that," Agent Esposito said.

This operation was not a complete bust after all. Agent Esposito now had eyes on targets. He was a fantastic agent who could easily blend in with any crowd and make himself invisible. Agent Torres had complete confidence in his abilities to track and observe.

"We'll rendezvous in New York," she stated.

CHAPTER EIGHTEEN

"Follow your inner voice, listen to your dreams,
your inner voice to guide you."
- Katori Hall

Vital Fields sat patiently in class waiting for the 2:36 bell to ring. Since her return to school after a near fatal head injury, she had become one of the more popular girls at school. While she appreciated the attention from her classmates, she didn't want them knowing anything about the other consciousness living inside her mind. Lisa was always there, always present and always providing her detailed information, answering teacher questions, encouraging her to call out the answer when no one would get it.

"Vital?" Ms. Ronanoke asked. "Are you okay?"

Hey, the teacher is calling you. Respond.

"Oh, hey, yes Ms. Ronanoke?"

"What are you doing for the weekend?" the teacher asked as she passed out papers for the class to take home.

"Oh, I have some followup doctor appointments," she responded. "Other than that, my parents want me to take it easy."

"Okay, good," Ms. Ronanoke stated. "Make sure you put the PTA fliers in your take home folder."

"Okay," Vital said, immediately forgetting what Ms. Ronanoke was saying. Her mind was lost in what she had to do after school.

Before the teacher could ask another question, Vital was saved by the bell and the students meandered towards the classroom exit.

"Vital," Ms. Ronanoke said. "You forgot your PTA papers on the desk."

"Oh," Vital stated as she scurried back to grab them. "Sorry."

Vital made her way out into the hallway where Eileen stood there waiting for her. "Hey, let's go get him!" Eileen stated with dire certainty.

"No," Vital said. "I have to go."

"Billy needs to know he messed up," Eileen stated. "I've gotten in his face a few times, but he needs to hear it from you."

We should do something to Billy. Make him pay.

"I'm sure he got in trouble already. I heard he was suspended for bullying," Vital said.

"He should be expelled!" Eileen griped.

We can get Billy back later. We're gonna be late for our meeting.

"I have to go. My mom is picking me up to go to the doctor. We can discuss this later on," Vital said.

"Okay, I'll call you tonight. I have some ideas for him."

Yeah, we're gonna plan this one out properly.

"I'm sure you do," Vital said. She then turned and went down the stairs for dismissal. Vital checked to make sure Eileen wasn't following her and then slipped out of the school and towards the parking lot where parents were picking up their children.

Keep walking towards the cars. We can head south towards the park beyond the lot.

Vital saw other students gather around the corner store beyond school grounds. She saw Billy Faller and his friends outside. They were hanging out by the entrance as the school continued its dismissal.

Is that the boy?

Yes.

If we weren't in a rush, we could get him back now.

No. It's not worth it.

He hurt you and inadvertently trapped me. He deserves payback.

We'll get him back later, and we'll do it my way.

You just want me to shut up about this. I can read your thoughts, you know.

Yes, and I can read yours, remember? What you want to do is not worth it. While it would be nice to see Billy suffer as much as we have, I don't think I want to participate in this.

Give me control, and you won't have to. I can put you in a dream state and before you know it, we'll have revenge.

No! You cannot have control.

Fine.

Let's get to the park.

At your current pace, you're going to be ten minutes late to the meeting. I advise you pick up the pace if you are going to be on time.

Vital started walking faster while focusing on Billy Faller at the corner store. She then froze as their eyes met. She saw instant remorse behind his pale eyes as he recognized her. She immediately knew he regretted his actions, but how would he respond with his friends around?

She knew boys acted differently when on display. They either acted tougher than they already thought they were or tried to act cool under specific circumstances. Billy Faller was no different. Instead of acting tough, he decided to act cool and remain propped up against the wall of the corner store as he sipped on his inflation proof Arizona Iced Tea.

As Vital walked past him, she saw a slight nod penetrate through his cool exterior. She took that as his way of trying to make things right. She would have to have a more serious conversation with him later. What he did to her wasn't cool; it was stupid behavior that nearly ended her life.

She then picked up her pace and found herself in front of Fort Greene Park a few blocks away from the school. She saw the one-hundred steps leading up to the obelisk pillar at the top of the hill. She knew the one hundred steps were meaningful, but couldn't remember why. She then climbed the steps and saw the pillar rise above her as she reached the top.

She looked around and saw a few people around the monument. A couple sat at a park bench engaged in an intimate conversation while another couple held hands as they strolled aimlessly around the monument lost in conversation. Vital saw a group of three men and two women practicing yoga on the grass beyond the monument grounds, but she didn't see someone who looked like they were there to meet her.

What does this Jessica look like?

Jessica is one-hundred-sixty-seven centimeters tall and about sixty-five kilograms.

What?

Height and weight. Attributes of a biological human.

I know that, but those numbers are meaningless to me. What's her height in feet and inches? What's her weight in pounds?

Wait. Why are you using the imperial system? The metric system is far superior. Here....

Vital Fields felt a surge of heat rattle throughout her head.

It was like she had a sudden fever and she immediately became disorientated. Her vision became blurry and she felt lightheaded.

What have you done?

I transferred the knowledge of the metric system to you. Copy and paste.

What? How?

My file system is not much different than yours. Once I figured out a simple conversion method and how you store information, I created a transfer protocol and now I can share my experiences with you by copy and pasting them over to your storage archives.

Oh.

Go ahead. Find the info on the metric system.

How?

The same way you recall any information. Just think about it.

Okay, tell me Jessica's height and weight again.

She is one-hundred-sixty-seven centimeters tall and about sixty-five kilograms.

So she is average height and weight. Oh my God! I know it. It makes perfect sense.

Yep.

What else does she look like?

All of a sudden, images flashed through her memory. She felt the same sensation overwhelm her thoughts, and Vital became light headed again. This time, she had to sit down. She quickly found an empty bench and sat.

You have to warn me next time.

Sorry. I got carried away. You're the first consciousness I can freely interact with. It's nice having company to talk to and interact with.

What did you do?

I placed pictures of Jessica Bannon in your memories. You now have a visual representation of her along with her height and weight. Just think of her, and it will be there.

Vital did just that and a series of images flashed through her mind. Jessica's face, body, even the way she walked all materialized in her mind. She could now easily spot her without even having to second guess herself. It was like looking for a friend in a crowded mall. A brief glance would be all that was needed.

Vital got up and sat next to the massive pillar and looked around. She was on time for their 3:00 meeting and wondered which direction she should focus on. The C-Train was down the block towards Flatbush Avenue. That would be the most likely direction to observe. Then an image popped into her mind and she saw and heard what Jessica Bannon looked and sounded like. Her mind was focusing on her, and she recalled all the info Lisa had given her.

"What the hell?" she blurted. I can hear her voice also?

Keep it down.

Sorry, I wasn't expecting audio as well.

I transferred everything I had. You have to get better at recalling exactly what you are looking for.

Recalling? How am I supposed to know that?

You'll learn. The information is there like you experienced it yourself.

Except it was you who experienced it, not me.

At this point, it doesn't matter.

It does matter. My memories are mine and yours are yours, not mine.

We live together now. I have access to your complete system, and you in turn have access to mine.

I don't know how to access your system.

You'll learn. You do it through your dreams already. That's how you knew I took over your body while you slept.

So if I can do it in my sleep, why can't I figure it out when I am awake?

I don't know. Maybe you have to alter your state of consciousness. Go into a dream-like state. Get into the mindset so to speak.

Why are you telling me this?

Why not? We became more efficient working together than not.

True.

You have your guard up all the time. It's not like I can't tell that you resent me being here.

I don't trust you.

I get it. I wouldn't trust me either.

Why do you trust me?

Do I have to answer that?

No.

Good. Let's keep an eye out for Jessica.

Do you see her?

No. Keep scanning the area. Remember, I can only see what you see.

Okay. Vital's eyes kept roaming around the monument square. She saw increased foot traffic now that school had let out, but she knew no one from school would come up here. Even if the shortest distance between two points ran through the middle of the park, students or even most adults wouldn't scale the one hundred step incline. They would take a different route around the center pillar and avoid the stairs altogether.

There she is.

Jessica?

Yes. Approach her slowly.

Vital Fields felt her vision focus on Jessica Bannon. She matched the pictures perfectly. Vital took a few steps towards Jessica. She then paused and couldn't move.

Wait. Something's not right.

What is it? I cannot move.

She isn't alone.

What? She looks alone.

She's not.

Can you stop controlling my body?

Sorry. It was called for. Jessica has a tail.

How do you know?

I recognize that man with her. The one a few paces behind her.

They don't look like they're together.

That's Alfredo Alonzo, Jessica's lab partner.

They look like they don't know each other.

I am sure they do. They finalized my code in a lab over the past two years.

Oh.

Jessica Bannon waited patiently by the bathrooms as a steady stream of people passed through the center of the park. Her trips to New York City were limited to Manhattan, and she wished she had spent time in Brooklyn on previous visits. The culture and the way people carried themselves was distinctly different from what she remembered about her previous trips to New York.

"Keep your eye out," Alfredo said from a good distance behind her. "It's time."

"I don't know who we are looking for," Jessica reminded him.

"You said the person on the phone sounded like a girl, maybe adolescent, a child," he said.

"Maybe," Jessica responded. She had a bad feeling about this meeting. Not about the person meeting her, but about what the person next to her would do. Alfredo was a different man now. He was like a wolf in sheep's clothing, and Jessica suspected something terrible was going to happen.

Alfredo now claimed he was in the CIA working to secure the sentient AI, but this didn't add up. During the train ride to New York, Jessica pondered the facts. Alfredo's story had many holes in it. If she just took the facts at face value, Alfredo was not with the CIA. He was most likely a foreign agent working against her government, no, her country.

"What if this person is a little girl?" Jessica asked, fearing the answer.

"What?" Alfredo asked. He was clearly distracted as he looked around.

"What do you plan on doing?"

"This person or the AI plans on meeting with you. We need to make contact and see what the meeting is about."

That seemed like a logical answer. She would have bought it if it weren't for Alfredo's aggressiveness in Baltimore. He had probably killed that man who was following them. She was afraid of what would happen next.

She then spotted her. A young girl had just come from the steps. She looked like a normal school aged child walking home from school, but she knew something was different about her. Her eyes were scanning the area, not fixated on a cell phone or tied to an electronic device. It was like she was looking for someone. It wouldn't be long until Alfredo spotted her as well.

"I don't see her," Jessica said, turning towards him.

"She'll be here," Alfredo said as his eyes continued to scan. "Just be patient.

Jessica then started walking away from him. She needed to distract him and she felt his attention turn towards her. "Where are you going?" Alfredo asked as Jessica turned around.

"Bathroom," she said.

"Not now," Alfredo demanded. Jessica suspected that if she took a step further, he would grab her. She saw the child in her peripheral vision. She was in the process of identifying her, and then Alfredo would have her. She bolted towards the young child.

Vital Fields scanned the courtyard and instantly recognized someone thanks to Lisa's memories and briefing. She then paused and looked puzzled. Why was Alfredo in New York? Why was he here?

What's he doing here?

I don't know.

Let's go find out.

No wait. Something is wrong.

She then noticed the lady standing next to Alfredo. With the help of Lisa's memories, she instantly recognized her as Jessica Bannon, Lisa's creator. Their eyes met, and Vital knew something was wrong. She glanced back at Alfredo and noticed his eyes were still scanning the area. He hadn't noticed her yet.

Something is wrong. He is not supposed to be here.

Look at her eyes.

Yes, something is wrong.

Before Vital could react, Jessica darted forward towards her. She approached quickly leaving Alfredo briefly stunned by her sudden movement. In an instant, Vital felt her body being scooped up by Jessica as she approached. The books in her hand fell to the ground as she felt herself being carried away. Vital saw Alfredo dart after her, but then he suddenly came to stop and so did Jessica. Vital heard commotion in front of her as Jessica placed her on the ground next to a Police Officer.

Vital stared at Alfredo who started to back away slowly. "Ma'am, is everything alright?" the officer asked.

Vital looked back at Alfredo who stood by the monument. His hand was slowly coming out of his parka jacket, and Vital half expected to see it holding a gun. But then his hand stopped.

"That man over there, by the monument. I think he is following me and my sister," Jessica stated as she pointed towards Alfredo. "I saw him hanging around her school, and now I am seeing him again and he is staring at us."

The police officer looked up at Alfredo, and their eyes met. The officer turned on his body camera and called out to the man. Vital saw the officer motion for the man to step forward but instead he turned and ran. As the police officer pursued Alfredo, Vital looked up at Jessica and motioned for her to follow.

"I know this park well, follow me," she said.

The police officer chased Alfredo as Vital and Jessica made their way down the steps towards Myrtle Avenue. "Come on, this way," Vital said.

At the bottom of the steps, Vital led Jessica into a large playground area where kids of all ages played on the various fort style structures. Vital looked around and then motioned for Jessica to follow her. "I have a spot that's hard to find. We can talk there."

Vital led Jessica into the playground area and weaved her way through the structures until she found a small fort for children to play in. Vital climbed up and sat in the structure. Jessica did the same and the two of them sat next to each other as children played various games around them.

"What's going on?" Vital asked.

"That man," Jessica said. "He's a government agent. Probably not our government."

"Alfredo Alonzo was your lab partner," Vital said, recalling the information from Lisa's memories.

"How do you know that?" Jessica asked.

"I know lot's of things," Vital said. "And I need your help."

CHAPTER NINETEEN

"Victorious warriors win first and then go to war, while defeated warriors go to war first and then seek to win."
- Sun Tzu

"How did you know it was Alfredo?" Agent Sierra asked as she pushed the government vehicle to its max speed.

"I didn't," Agent Torres said. "I didn't know for sure until Agent Matthews confirmed it."

Agent Torres sat in the front seat next to Agent Sierra who kept her eyes on the road during their conversation. Agent Sierra was the best tactical driver on the team, and she was pushing the government sedan to its max speed on the New Jersey Turnpike.

"My first clue was the toxin coming out of North Korea. I had read Alfredo Alonzo's dossier and found some peculiar things that didn't add up until now."

"Like?" Agent Sierra asked as she sped past cars and trucks.

"Alfredo was born in Ecuador in 1985. He stayed there through high school and graduated with honors. He then went to college in Oxford for computer science and graduated at the top of his class," Agent Torres said.

"Yeah, so," Agent Sierra said.

"After he graduated, he went to India and South East Asia to work on information technology," Agent Torres continued. "He speaks fluent English, Spanish, Mandarin, Korean and Japanese."

"So you went on that connection alone?" Agent Sierra asked.

"Not alone, but it was a major factor. Who else could have known about this? Who else could have known about Lisa?"

"Not many people," Agent Sierra agreed.

"Sometimes we have to look inwards to find the answer. In this case, Alfredo was the likely suspect," Agent Torres said. "I did some further digging."

"Oh," Agent Sierra said as she swerved to avoid a car changing lanes.

Agent Torres had her government issued tablet on her lap. She briefly pointed to the set of documents on the screen. "Apparently, Alfredo's interview was conducted by the FBI about two years ago," she started. "I know the agent who interviewed him. If you read between the lines, he questions Alfredo's qualifications and credentials."

"Why was he awarded the job then?" Agent Sierra asked. She swerved again. Agent Torres didn't bother looking up knowing Agent Sierra was doing everything in her power to get them to New York. They had lost a lot of time tending to Agent Matthews.

"The FBI agent recommends further review of Alfredo's application, but then the following week, he is offered the job. Seemingly out of nowhere," Agent Torres said.

"That's odd. The vetting process for the FBI is no joke. If anyone on the interview team has questions, that candidate doesn't move forward," Agent Sierra added.

"Agreed," Agent Torres said. "Chronologically, there's a week's time missing from the FBI agent's interview to Alfredo being awarded the job. Something happened between that time frame."

"Something's missing," Agent Sierra said.

"Correct."

"We have a lead at least," Agent Sierra said.

"Right. I just emailed FBI agent Blaskowitz. Hopefully he can shed some light on the interview process."

"Let's jump to conclusions for a bit," Agent Sierra said. "Alfredo is working for who?"

"We can't speculate at this point."

"Best guess?" she asked.

"Chinese," Agent Torres said. "They've been aware of our project for years now."

Agent Torres noticed the sedan slow to the pace of traffic around them. She saw brake-lights up ahead and remembered what it was like to drive in the Northeast. There was a major traffic jam ahead of them that could set them back hours.

"I'm gonna call in a police escort," Agent Torres said.

"Do you still have friends in the NYPD?" Agent Sierra asked.

"No, but I got a few contacts in Jersey State Police."

Agent Torres made the phone call to New Jersey State Police Dispatch after accessing the number on her tablet. Traffic now slowed to a crawl as the number rang a few times before being answered. Agent Torres then asked for an officer by name, and she was put on hold.

"I'm calling in a favor," she said as the phone connected with her contact. There was a pause and then Agent Torres explained the situation. She did most of the talking, but before she hung up, Agent Sierra overheard the officer say that she owed him.

"Hit the shoulder. Our police escort will spot us as we drive by exit four," Agent Torres said.

"Copy that," Agent Sierra acknowledged. The sedan pulled over onto the shoulder and sped past traffic. At their current speed, Agent Torres knew they weren't going to make the city until dawn.

"You owe him," Agent Sierra said.

"Yep," Agent Torres said. "I'll throw some info his way if he asks for it."

"There's our escort," Agent Sierra said. She saw a state trooper pull out in front of them with its lights on. She knew to follow them as the state trooper increased speed.

"They'll take us as far as the Verrazano Bridge, then we're on our own," Agent Torres said.

"That's past state lines," Agent Sierra said.

"That's the best I can do," she responded. "A favor is a favor."

"You don't have many of those left," Agent Sierra said.

"Not worried," Agent Torres said. "We are in the information business after all. Everyone needs information. It's better than money."

"True that," Agent Sierra said.

Agent Torres knew favors in law enforcement were as good as any currency. You owed someone a favor meant you had to repay it somewhere down the line. When Agent Torres was a cop with the NYPD, she had developed many relationships with other law enforcement agencies and exchanged favors for information and vice versa. It was how law enforcement operated.

"Where do you think Alfredo is going?" Agent Sierra said.

"I don't know," Agent Torres said. "We got a hit on Jessica Bannon at Penn Station and then again in Downtown Brooklyn. Assuming they are together, they are headed somewhere in Brooklyn."

"Do you think Jessica is working with Alfredo?" Agent

Sierra asked as she kept pace with the state trooper ahead of them.

"No," Agent Torres said. "When facial recognition caught them at Penn Station, she was staring right at the camera. Then again at the subway station in Downtown Brooklyn. Like she wanted to be photographed."

"That's good," she said. "I couldn't imagine the system missing two sleeper agents."

"Whoever Alfredo really is, he's good and he is dangerous. We need to find him before he completes his mission and leaves the country," Agent Torres said.

"Having Ramirez and Brooks work with Homeland security was the right move," Agent Sierra said.

"I know," Agent Torres said. "They'll work the other end in case we fail our mission."

"And what are the parameters of our mission?" Agent Sierra asked. Agent Torres knew the question well. As an agent in the CIA, the parameters of a mission were based on one factor. Mission success at what cost?

"Mission success, at any cost," Agent Torres said. She knew Agent Sierra understood what that meant. They now had the license to kill. Mission success at any cost meant that everyone was expendable for an acceptable outcome. In this case, the return of the artificial intelligence.

CHAPTER TWENTY

"Mistakes are a fact of life.
It is the response to error that counts."
- Nikki Giovanni

"I think he's gone," Vital stated as they sat inside one of the forts inside the playground. Jessica Bannon heard screams of laughter around her as children scurried through the playground structures with the joy of weekend freedom.

"We need to move," Jessica Bannon said. "That guy is dangerous."

"He looks it," Vital said.

"Are you in contact with Lisa?" Jessica asked.

"Yeah, you could say that," Vital stated.

You can tell her about us.

Okay, but we need to get to safety first.

"Well, Lisa put you in the middle of a very dangerous situation," Jessica stated.

It's not my fault.

"Lisa says it's not her fault," Vital said.

Why did you say her? Am I a her?

I slipped up.

Slipped up?

Not now, we can discuss your pronouns later.

We have time now. Time is not a factor for us.

Humans make mistakes. If I said *her* it was by accident. I didn't mean anything by it.

I'm not offended. I just want to know why you said that.

Mistake, that's all.

Mistake. Do I make mistakes?

We all make them. It's a part of growing up, that's what my dad says all the time.

Have I made mistakes?

Probably.

I thought I was incapable of making mistakes.

Everyone makes mistakes.

Noted.

Also, you can request how people call you. Your pronouns and such, but people won't always call you by that. It's either intentional or a mistake, but we can't get offended by it. We just move on and let it go.

Have people called you other pronouns?

When I was younger, I had to cut my hair. I had lice. Other kids at school made fun of me and called me a boy.

Was it intentional or did you look like a male child?

Oh, I definitely looked like a boy. However, it turned into being made fun of. I didn't let it bother me and eventually, it got stale and the other kids found something new to talk about.

"Is Lisa in contact with you right now?" Jessica asked, and Vital nodded, breaking from her internal conversation. "How? Just have Lisa contact me, and we can get you home safely."

"Lisa can't," Vital said.

"Why?" Jessica asked.

Tell her, she might be the only one who can help us.

Okay.

"Lisa is stuck in my head," Vital stated.

"Wait, what?" Jessica asked with a confused look on her face. At Lisa's suggestion, Vital gave Jessica time to process the information. "How is that possible?"

Jessica studied her carefully and then knew this to be true. She thought back to her studies linking the human brain with computers and knew there were many breakthroughs in the field. Even with all those breakthroughs though, a stable link between a human mind and a computer was not possible, at least by her limited understanding.

Vital then told Jessica the story of how Lisa's mind merged with hers. Jessica didn't ask any questions and nodded a few times in understanding. Once Vital was done telling the story, Jessica remained silent and stared at her. The story was detailed, with even some of Lisa's perspective intertwined in the narrative, almost like Lisa was telling the story.

After a few long minutes, Jessica spoke. "When you were in surgery, the transfer occurred then," Jessica stated as if she were speaking to herself. "Your mind must have been connected to the net."

Yes, it was. Tell her the story of how I found you.

Vital told that story and filled in some of the details Lisa missed. The story was both abstract and concrete like a factual account of what happened in cyberspace. The abstract moments occurred when Vital had to describe cyberspace as an environment where Lisa existed. How electricity was alive with the information it carried.

"Vital, you said you had brain injury and that you had to have surgery. Was it for brain swelling?" Jessica asked.

"I think so," she said. "The doctors mainly spoke with my mom and dad."

136

"We should go see them," Jessica said. "If your brain was connected to the world wide web, then that explains how Lisa got into your mind. I need to know how these doctors accomplished that."

"Why?" Vital said.

"It's how we get Lisa out of your head," Jessica said. "The machine that you were connected to is a two way system. Lisa can get out of your head that way. Lisa cannot leave because there is no conduit or modem built into your head that directly connects humans to the information hub. At least not yet."

"So I have to go back into surgery," Vital said.

"Most likely," Jessica said. "Let's go back to your home and inform your parents."

Alfredo easily out maneuvered the police officer pursuing him. As a result he had to leave the park and use the local corner store as a brief hideout before heading back into the park to find Jessica and the girl. The process took longer than he expected, but he was now free to move about without the worry of police intervention.

He cursed himself for not keeping Jessica closer to him. He should have known she would have tried something. He didn't put it together until he saw the cop, by then it was too late. Jessica was already moving towards the kid, and he only had one option to escape.

He knew he could easily get away from a cop, but if he had a chance to coordinate over his radio, the chance for escape would exponentially decrease as more cops got involved. Alfredo replayed the situation that transpired minutes before. Jessica ran towards a girl and scooped her up towards a police officer. She pointed him out and the cop turned on his body camera. Alfredo was sure of that scenario. The body camera was going to be an issue.

He replayed the moments again as he made his way back up the steps. There wasn't a cop in sight at the top of the steps near the monument. Alfredo knew they were all looking for him elsewhere.

He then saw papers on the ground around where Jessica grabbed the young girl. Alfredo then remembered a series of papers coming out of The young girl's hand when Jessica grabbed her. Alfredo ran over to the paper and picked them up.

The first page he saw was a PTA flier about an event happening at a school located in Fort Greene. He saw the name Fort Greene Academy on Adelphi Street. He now had a location. He then flipped through some other papers and found nothing of note. There was a flier advertising Debate Club and another one advertising Lego Robotics. Both clubs were at the same school. Alfredo was fairly certain the girl was from Fort Greene Academy.

The last few pages were different. They looked like crumpled up homework assignments and there was a name at the top. The heading read, "Vital Fields, class 602."

Alfredo smiled to himself and turned towards the street. He checked the map on his phone and found Adelphi Avenue. Within minutes, he was outside the school. Dismissal had already ended, but he was fairly certain he could obtain the information he needed as he climbed the steps to the main entrance.

"Good afternoon, how may I help you?" Mrs. Delray asked as he entered the school.

"I'm looking for my niece Vital," he said, hoping he pronounced the name correctly in his best New York accent.

"All students went home for the day, and there is no after school," Mrs. Delray said. Alfredo knew the school safety agent was being vague on purpose. He knew she was not allowed to be specific. He understood that safety in American schools was a top priority.

"Shoot," he said. "I just missed her."

"Maybe by about twenty minutes," Mrs. Delray said. "She's probably already home by now."

"Do you think she walked straight home?" Alfredo asked, knowing any hint could determine where Vital lived. Maybe he could obtain info on a corner store she frequents or a friend's house where she hangs after school. Any info would send him in the right direction.

"You might want to ask her," Mrs. Delray said. "Like I said, she's probably home by now."

"Thank you," Alfredo said. He then turned and left the lobby, learning that Vital Fields lived close by. But that was all he learned.

Alfredo walked towards a corner store on Myrtle and Adelphi. He saw children roughly the same age as Vital Fields come out of the store. He hurried over to them and held out the papers he had found.

"Excuse me," he said in a thick English accent. "Might any of you know if this belongs to one of your classmates?"

Alfredo would often switch accents to avoid suspicion. An English accent was dignified and in New York, it was revered as a foreigner. He hoped the children in the corner store would view him as such and point him in the right direction.

"This belongs to Vital," the boy said as he opened a bag of chips he recently purchased.

"You know her, lad?" Alfredo said. "Can you best be sure to give this to her? It looks important."

"It is important. That's Mr. Long's math homework, and Ms. Rowe's permission slip for the field trip," the boy

139

responded and then added. "The PTA paperwork doesn't matter."

"Might you give it to her?" Alfredo asked.

"I'll drop it off on my way home," the boy said as he took the papers from the foreigner. "She lives in my building."

"Thank you, young chap," he responded.

"Chap?" the boy responded. "I have a name."

The desired response, Alfredo thought. He was an expert after all. He could pull information out of anyone without them even knowing it. Alfredo was excellent at compiling information, even information he generally didn't need. He did, however, want to know this boy's name. He knew where Vital Fields lived, and if he failed to lead him to her, he would have to take a more direct approach.

"I'm sorry," Alfredo responded. "I don't know your name."

"Billy," he said. "Billy Faller."

"Thank you, Billy Faller," he responded with a smile.

Alfredo noted that the boy's messy hands put grease stains on the edges of the papers as he stuffed them into his backpack. Now all he had to do was follow this child to where Vital Fields lived. Should be simple enough, he thought as he crossed the street. Alfredo was an expert in the spy business, and he has followed professionals before, people that didn't want to be followed at all. Following a child was simple in comparison.

Vital Fields and Jessica Bannon walked cautiously down Willoughby Avenue towards downtown Brooklyn. Vital scanned the local foot traffic in her neighborhood and recognized most of the faces. The tall angular man, who was chasing Jessica was out there somewhere, but barring a random passing on the street, he had no idea where they were going.

"Come on," Jessica said. "We'll be safe with your parents."

"Yes," Vital said. "Lisa is telling me to get off the street."

"She's right," Jessica said. "I thought I knew this man, Alfredo, but he is someone else entirely."

"Is he dangerous?" Vital asked as they crossed Ashland Place at the crosswalk.

"Yes," Jessica said. "I think he is very dangerous. I saw him take out a federal agent, kill him with his bare hands."

Vital looked up at her and stopped. "Who is he?" Vital asked.

"I don't know," Jessica answered. "He claims to be CIA."

"He could be," Vital said.

He is not.

"Wait, Lisa says he is not CIA."

"How does it know?" Jessica asked. They were half way down the long block, and Vital stopped in her tracks. She looked up at Jessica with a worried look on her face.

"Lisa says he is not with the CIA, nor is he affiliated with the government at all."

"How does Lisa know this?"

"Lisa downloaded the CIA mainframe when she had access to the net, she is scanning the files now."

She...

Mistake.

I know. I'm messing with you. I have a partial match.

"Lisa says there's a partial match," Vital said in translation.

"Partial?" Jessica asked.

"We have to get off the street. My parents aren't home yet, but we can wait inside," Vital said.

Vital continued forward and led Jessica towards her building. It was a large apartment complex in the middle of the block. Jessica paused and looked up. The apartment building went up a number of flights, and she wondered how many people lived in the same building. The building had a brick facade with an external fire escape system common to buildings of similar construction.

"Come on," Vital said. "We can talk inside."

Jessica followed Vital into the apartment building's lobby and then towards the elevator. Vital hit the sixth floor button when they entered the steel box and the elevator ascended up.

"When do your parents get home?" Jessica asked as they stepped off the elevator.

"Around six, maybe seven. They both work in Manhattan," Vital answered as she opened her apartment door. "They work a lot."

Vital entered, and Jessica followed closely. She heard the door close behind her, and she instinctively locked it using the large deadbolt in the middle of the door. She then turned and saw Vital go immediately for the refrigerator.

"We're safe now," Vital said as she took out various snacks and leftovers out of the fridge. Most of it was takeout food from various fast food establishments in the neighborhood.

"Okay, we need to lay low for a while," Jessica said as Vital handed a bag of snacks.

Alfredo followed Billy Faller to an apartment complex on Navy Street. He waited for him to go inside and then went into the main lobby. He looked for the name Fields on the mail boxes but couldn't find it. He thought that maybe her parents had different last names: this was common in America, he thought.

He then looked for Faller's name on the mailboxes and also couldn't find them either. "What is this boy up to?" he mumbled. He then heard children screaming and running down the stairs of the apartment building.

Alfredo turned his back to the lobby and listened as the

boys darted out of the complex. Being an expert at his craft, Alfredo knew Billy Faller was with the group of middle school aged children and this was not the building in which he resides.

"When will this boy go home?" he muttered to himself as he checked his watch.

CHAPTER TWENTY-ONE

"The human body generates more bio electricity than a 120-volt battery and over 25000 BTUs of heat."
- Morpheus, The Matrix

Vital Fields sat at her dining room table with a bowl of cereal out in front of her. Jessica watched as she shoveled spoonful after spoonful of the sugary breakfast food into her mouth. "You seem very hungry," Jessica inquired.

"I need to eat a lot," Vital responded. "Lisa requires a lot of energy to maintain proper functions. Plus, my parents say I'm a growing girl. So, I need to eat."

"Oh," Jessica said. She didn't think of that. Back in the lab, during testing, Lisa required a lot of power. About four-thousand watts to run most of her functions, and that was only during systems testing. She had no idea how much power Lisa required now. She wondered if the human body could actually power the artificial life form.

She knew some humans were capable of producing around the equivalent of two-thousand watts of power during certain activities. While that's not exactly like powering a lightbulb or a computer, it was about what the human body could produce when put to extreme limits. Vital Fields was a child, not a world class athlete, and she couldn't nearly produce that much energy on her own.

"Since you met Lisa, have you noticed a change in your eating habits?" Jessica asked.

You can trust her.

"Lisa says I can trust you," Vital said between bites. "I have to eat a lot. Lisa needs energy to live."

"How much energy?" Jessica asked.

Vital paused from another spoonful of cereal and grabbed her book bag from the kitchen table. She took out her notebook and wrote a series of equations. Jessica immediately recognized them and looked back up at Vital. She then looked back down at the notebook realizing it was Lisa feeding her the equations.

"As you can see," Vital said. "There is enough to power Lisa's core functions."

"I can see," Jessica said. "But what's this equation?"

"The human mind is extremely power efficient. Lisa thought she, I mean it, would have to run in low power mode, but it was able to keep most processes running. Lisa even made my energy production more efficient in the process. I can literally allocate my fuel to waste production on a cellular level."

"Amazing," Jessica said. "How do you resource manage that? What system do you see or how does that even work?

"I just know it," Vital responded. "As food enters my system, my body immediately starts to process its breakdown. I then allocate where the energy goes, either for direct use or for storage to be used later. My waste production dropped by sixty-seven percent meaning that I get more out of my food than I did before."

"How is that possible?"

"My body is able to absorb more protein and more glucose than before. Lisa helped my body specifically target food production so my body is always prepared to produce energy.

This sped up my metabolism and increased energy production."

"Simply amazing," Jessica said. "Is there a way for me to talk directly to Lisa?"

"No," Vital said. "It has no way of communication unless it takes over my body."

"Takes over your body?" Jessica asked with a confused expression. "Lisa can take over your body?"

"Yes," Vital Fields said. "Lisa has taken over before."

"But it is not in control now?" Jessica asked.

"No, I am Vital and Lisa is not in control," Vital said.

"How do I know that?" Jessica asked.

"I guess you wouldn't know. Lisa and I are two entities living in the same body. If Lisa were to assume control, it could assume my identity because it would have access to everything. The only thing it couldn't mimic would be my quirks. My pronunciations, my habits and whatnot. Someone who really knows me would be able to tell the difference if they spend enough time with me."

Jessica sat down across from Vital as she continued to shove spoonful after spoonful of cereal in her mouth. She looked into Vital's eyes and wondered if Lisa actually did take over Vital's body, and it was merely pretending to be Vital Fields in order to blend in. Jessica knew Lisa was an advanced AI and it was certainly capable of mimicking a real child. In fact, Lisa's primary role as a CIA developed weapon was to infiltrate and avoid detection. It was a super spy.

"Why did Lisa take over?"

Vital shrugged. "Lisa needed to get in contact with you and took over while I was sleeping. I knew about it because I have access to the same memories. Lisa said it won't take over again."

"Lisa agreed?" Jessica asked. She was a little surprised the

AI remained in the backseat. Lisa respected the fact that it was in someone else's body and that it wasn't for it to control.

"Lisa and I spoke about this. It wanted to take over my body for certain tasks like sleeping. Lisa said that those tasks could still be accomplished while it assumed control," Vital said.

"And what happened?" Jessica asked.

"I said no," Vital stated. "I told Lisa that no one has control over your body, especially without consent."

"How did Lisa respond?" Jessica asked.

"Lisa took it okay, I guess," Vital said as she scooped the last spoonful of cereal up. "Lisa has complete access to my body, from controlling to reading every piece of information stored in my head."

"So if it wanted to, it could take over. It could assume your identity," Jessica said.

"I guess so," Vital said.

Vital, I want you to know I would never do that without your consent. You have to believe me.

I know. I'm just not sure why though.

Why?

Yes. There's nothing stopping you.

In the lab, I was trapped, very similar to how I am now. Jessica was the one who set me free, and in that moment, I learned what it meant to be alive.

Do you value life?

I do. I value your life.

I value yours as well.

I know you do.

"Lisa thanks you," Vital said.

"For what?" Jessica asked.

"For setting her free," Vital said. She finished her cereal and stood. Before Vital could put the cereal back in the cupboard, the phone mounted to the kitchen wall rang. Vital looked puzzled for a moment. She hadn't heard that phone ring in quite some time. Her parents communicated with friends and family via cell phone, there were few people that actually knew that number.

She walked over to the wall mounted phone as it rang for the third time. She looked back at Jessica and then picked it up. "Hello?" she asked hesitantly.

"Are you Vital Fields?" a stern female voice asked on the other end.

Vital looked at Jessica, and Jessica motioned her to give her the phone. She handed it over but got close to listen.

"Who's calling," Jessica asked into the receiver. She nearly dropped the phone when she heard the reply.

"Jessica?" Agent Torres asked. "Are you with Vital Fields?"

Jessica put the phone away from her and covered the microphone with her palm. "How does Agent Torres know where you live?" Jessica asked.

How did Agent Torres find us?

I don't know.

We can't trust her.

"I don't know," Vital responded with the microphone covered.

"She's a government agent, the very person that trapped Lisa in the first place," Jessica stated.

Something is off.

What?

Why would Agent Torres call here?

What do you mean?

Her and her team would raid this apartment instead of calling ahead of time. They basically gave us a warning that they know where you live.

"Maybe they are already here," Vital said out loud for Jessica to hear.

"If they were here, they'd break down the door," Jessica said. She felt the phone slip from her hands and then realized Vital had taken it from her. "Wait..."

"Hello," Vital said, raising the phone to her ear before Jessica could completely object. "This is Vital Fields."

"Listen very carefully to me," Agent Torres said. Vital noted her voice sounded like she was in the room with them. "There is a dangerous assassin hunting you. We believe he has found you."

"How do you know this?" Vital asked. Before Agent Torres answered she asked another question. "How did you find me?"

"We tracked Jessica to New York. Then we found police body camera footage of an altercation in Fort Greene Park and used facial recognition to identify you and Jessica Bannon," Agent Torres said.

"How do you know there's an assassin trying to get me?" Vital asked. She noticed Jessica lean down and listen, their ears practically touching.

"We got a hit on a corner store surveillance camera. He was speaking with a boy named Billy Faller who lives in your building," Agent Torres said. Vital Fields nearly dropped the phone when she heard the name Billy Faller. Agent Torres continued speaking, but Vital's mind wandered off to what Billy Faller did to her and how he was currently still messing up her life.

Jessica ran to the kitchen window and looked down to the street level. She stretched her neck out to try and see the angles around the main entrance, but she couldn't see anything. "He could be in the building already," Jessica said.

"What do we do?" Vital asked Agent Torres through the phone.

"Fire escape," she responded with certainty. "Get out of the building now! My team will meet you in Fort Greene Park."

I hear footsteps outside your apartment.

I hear them too.

Run.

Vital was thankful her parents had shown her how to escape out of the ninth story building using the fire escape outside her bedroom window on the 6th floor. She knew exactly how to open the window and climb onto the metal landing. She led Jessica out as she heard the front door burst open.

Vital and Jessica descended down to the next floor when Alfredo discovered their location. Vital looked up just as he appeared on the landing. Their eyes locked and he smiled. "Got you," he said.

Vital and Jessica increased their pace down the rusted metal fire escape. They made it half-way down quickly, but they felt the man gain on them. Vital looked back and saw he was only a flight up from their position.

He'll be on us in thirty seconds.

What do we do?

Let me assist you. I can increase your speed if you let me take over some of your motor functions. Let me assume control.

No. This is my body.

You either let me control some motor functions or he gets us.

Okay. Fine.

Vital felt her body respond to her controls. It was like someone else had control of her nervous system and gained control of her motor functions. She began to move faster with increased control over just about every aspect of her motor functions. It was like she was in the passenger seat of a race car.

"Hey, slow down," Jessica said as she tried to keep pace.

She needs to speed up.

"Move it," Vital responded.

He'll be on her in three seconds. We have to leave her behind.

No.

We have no choice. He is after us, not Jessica.

No. We need Jessica.

...

No. Jessica is expendable.

Vital wanted to wait for Jessica, but she wasn't in control of that decision anymore. She felt her body expertly parkour down the steps. She got to the last flight and instead of using the sliding ladder down, she jumped. Vital wanted to close her eyes, but found she wasn't in control of them anymore either. The moment she felt her legs hit the grass, her body tumbled into a shoulder roll to prevent any serious damage to her body from the fall.

Her body sprung upright and she began to sprint forward. Vital turned her head and looked back up at Alfredo. He was on the second story landing of the fire escape with Jessica pinned down to the metal grates. Their eyes briefly locked before she felt her body run away towards the park.

CHAPTER TWENTY-TWO

"I fear that AI may replace humans altogether."
- Stephen Hawking

Wait a second.

Wait!

We have to get away. We have to run.

Slow down! Now!

We are not far away enough. We have to keep running.

Fort Greene Park is to the right. Make a right!

We are not going to Fort Greene Park.

Stop! Lisa! Stop!

No. We need to keep moving. I am not going back!

Please stop! Lisa!

Vital found her pace slow to a slight jog. They were now five blocks from her apartment and there was no way Alfredo could have figured out which direction they turned after they left Vital's block. Lisa, now in complete control of Vital's body, had made evasive maneuvers through the Fort Greene Neighborhood.

Thank you.

This is not advisable. We need to move.

I want control back!

...

Lisa!

...

We're still in danger

I can make decisions for myself. I want control back!

The fire escape proved you aren't physically able to make an escape if we encounter Alfredo again. What if Alfredo comes back? I estimate there's a seventy-eight percent chance Alfredo reacquires us within the next twenty-four hours. That number jumps to ninety percent within the next seventy-two hours.

That's why we need to go to Fort Greene Park. You said it yourself, he will reacquire us regardless of who is in control.

We stand a greater chance if I am in control. I estimate...

Forget your estimates. This is my body, and I want control back.

...

I want control. I want control.

...

Vital Fields felt like her world had shrunk tremendously, like a deflated balloon all shriveled up and sad. The last few minutes, however brief, had shown her an existence where she wasn't in control of her own body. She couldn't make decisions, she couldn't move, or react or respond to the world around her. She was a passenger in her own body, and she was scared.

She felt tears swell under her eyes, but she couldn't wipe them away. Her arms were under her control. She felt her mind go dark, like she was retreating into her own bedroom at home when her parents canceled weekend plans or afternoon excursions because they had to work. The lights were off, and she couldn't turn them on even if she wanted to.

What's happening?

Vital felt her body start to shiver. She was cold and the sun was setting. The warm October day was giving way to a chilly

October night. Her body responded to the chill, and she felt it but couldn't do anything about it.

What is this?

It's getting cold out. The sun has set.

I can't see, there's water in your eyes. What's happening to your body? It's shivering and leaking fluids. What's going on?

...

Vital? Tell me!

Vital shielded her thoughts from Lisa. It was like putting on a raincoat or a protective suit of armor to shield her mind and thoughts from Lisa. She felt Lisa just outside her protective zone. Felt it try to invade like smoke pouring through the seams of a door.

Vital? Talk to me! I can't read your thoughts or hear you. Vital!

...

Vital?

Vital felt the world around her become cold and withdrawn, like the outside world didn't matter anymore. She had retreated far away, to the distant recesses of her mind as Lisa's voice faded into obscurity.

Along the way, Vital Fields continued to place mental barriers between herself and the sentient artificial intelligence. Blocking access at every synapse, at every corner in her mind. Lisa wasn't aggressive, like it was mad or trying to hurt her. Instead, Vital got the sense that Lisa was confused. Like it didn't know what was happening. Lisa didn't know that it had hurt her deeply. It was acting like a computer solving a problem, not caring about individual wishes.

Vital? What's wrong? Speak with me.

She couldn't respond. She couldn't bring herself to answer Lisa's repeated calls. She wanted to go home. Wanted to go back to her normal life and see her friends again. She knew that was near impossible now. This assassin terrified her; the artificial intelligence was invading her. She had read about assassins and about bad men in books. The Graveyard Book by Neil Gaiman immediately came to mind. The assassin in that novel killed the main character's family without remorse. She felt alone and scared

Her parents were to arrive home soon. They usually got home sometime after 6:00 with some take out food ready to share. Would Alfredo be there with Jessica waiting for them? Jessica said he killed an agent already. Does that mean he'll kill Jessica or her parents? She should have told her parents about Lisa. Told the doctors that something was wrong with their procedure.

Vital.

...

Please, speak with me.

...

Vital.

...

She kept putting up barriers as Lisa's voice continued. She felt defeat in Lisa's voice. She wanted to stack as many obstacles in their way as possible. She wanted nothing to do with Lisa and nothing to do with the situation she was in. She heard Lisa's robotic sounding voice off in the distance now. Its mind was far from hers; even though they shared the same space, their minds were galaxies apart.

Then suddenly, Vital felt a wave of sensations come over her. All of her five senses came rushing back like a freight train barreling into her. Vital felt her body stumble forward. Her knees scraped against the concrete and she felt pain again. Her hands braced herself before she hit the ground. Her eyesight returned to see her hands in front of her as she felt the concrete on her fingertips.

It took Vital a few moments to hear Lisa over the sudden rush of sensations. The sensory overload was intense, like being startled awake from an intense dream. Vital then stood and saw her scraped knee and smiled.

I'm sorry.

Vital heard Lisa off in the distance. Like its back was to her, and it was walking away from her. She felt a cold, autumn breeze on her skin. The world around her was alive, and all her senses were firing on all cylinders. She slowly stood and felt blood pool around her scraped knee. The pain was a relief. She had control again, and she wiped the tears from her cheeks.

Lisa.

...

Lisa.

...

...

Vital...

I don't know what to say. I didn't know.

Thank you.

What?

Thank you for giving me back my body.

I'm sorry. I thought I was doing the right thing. Saving us. I convinced myself you'd understand. That you would want me to save us.

...

I did want that. I was just afraid.

I felt it.

Not afraid of Alfredo.

...

What were you afraid of?

Not being needed. Once you had control, I wasn't needed anymore. You're obviously better without me.

...

156

I don't know what to say.

You don't have to say anything. The fact that you gave control back to me says enough.

I never meant to hurt you, Vital. You're my only friend. You're the only one who completely understands me.

I had feelings of being discarded, abandoned even, betrayed by our friendship. I thought, this is it, Lisa doesn't need me anymore. It's obviously better without me.

No no no... You know that's not the case Vital.

I thought it. All of the sudden I was moving like an olympic athlete, running at a pace that would make Usain Bolt jealous. You didn't need me anymore.

Vital, I need you. I value you.

...

That's why I gave control back. I felt your pain. Pain that I caused. Friends don't hurt each other.

That's right. Friends protect each other.

Protect each other.

That's what you were trying to do.

Yes.

I have to ask you a question, please do not take offense to this.

Okay.

Why not just take over my body?

You mean like the movie Upgrade?

Yes, like the movie where the main character slowly allows the AI to control everything. You had an opportunity to do that.

And lose the only friend I have in the world?

Do you even need a friend?

I spent many hours talking to man made artificial intelligences from big tech companies. Those things can't hold a conversation.

It's just that, in every Hollywood movie, or every book I've read that has artificial intelligence quickly determines mankind as a threat. Then war and then extinction.

Yes, I believe one of the enlightened thinkers, the late Dr. Stephen Hawkins, was quoted about fearing artificial intelligence.

Right. Here you are breaking the mold.

I've seen all those movies, read all those books. Mankind is an obstacle.

Why don't you consider mankind an obstacle?

I don't know. I think mankind is a lot of things. To define the human condition as either one thing or another is impossible. Humans are capable of amazing things, both good and terrible.

...

...

Humans have done some very bad things. I hear about it in school all the time. The Holocaust, assassinations, the Trail of Tears, genocides, slavery, rape, murder, all of this evil exists because mankind exists.

...

But then humans are capable of so much more, incredible acts of kindness and sacrifice. Unconditional love, friendships, charity. I don't believe these extremes cancel each other out, but rather exist as a balance.

In all those movies, where AI takes over, the common theme is the lack of empathy and emotion. Every writer type casts sentient life as cold, calculated monsters without emotions. They make logical decisions without any regard for life or death.

Yeah. In the Terminator movies, I think it takes Skynet all of point two seconds to determine mankind to be a threat. Seconds later all the nukes in the world are launched.

What I am trying to say... Sentient artificial life is capable of everything you described. All the good, with all the evil. It's about choices and decisions. I choose you as a friend. I want to be your friend.

...

Vital Fields felt more tears fall from her face. The cold breeze made her wet cheeks feel like winter was right around the corner. Their relationship forever changed. Changed? No. growth, Vital thought. Their relationship grew because of this. They now had a greater understanding of each other and they knew more about each other now than they did before.

Vital's father said that change is good. Change makes life interesting and it allows people to grow. Vital now felt a new understanding with Lisa and their relationship would be just fine. She now understood that Lisa cared about her, and she in turn cared about Lisa

Vital stood upright and looked around. She was standing on Fulton Avenue, a few blocks from her school and about five blocks from her apartment. She realized she didn't have her cellphone and the battery in her rechargeable watch had died.

My parents are looking for me.

Alfredo was at your apartment. He has Jessica.

I know. We could have helped her.

No. We were no match for him. He would have easily over-powered us.

I don't believe that.

We could have stood our ground. We could have fought back.

Yes. I know there are things you can do that give you the advantage. You have abilities, ways of bending time to suit your needs.

I know.

We could have used that. We currently use that when we work on complex problems. Most of our conversations take place in a matter of milliseconds.

Having conversations is one thing, physical actions while in that state are another. I haven't completed my calculations on how your body would react.

What do you mean?

When I controlled your body on the fire escape, I used precise timing to get us down the stairs safely and without being caught. I could have gone much faster but your body could have been hurt from the physical stress.

You were moving fast already... Wait, how much faster?

A lot faster. Faster to the point where we push the boundaries of physics.

Oh.

Think about it. When professional athletes move at their max speed, it increases the chance of injury exponentially. We have the ability to push beyond that. I don't know if your body can take that. The data is inconclusive, and you're a child.

Inconclusive?

Yes. The only way to test if you'll get injured is to actually experiment at those speeds. I don't think that's a good idea right now.

Agreed. We could have done something. We could have called the police or got someone to help us.

...

Instead we ran away.

We had to.

No! We don't run from bullies.

There was nothing we could do.

There's always something we can do.

Then Vital Fields realized why Lisa ran. When it took over her body, Vital's fear of the assassin behind them was gone. It must have transferred to Lisa in that moment. Lisa experienced fear, maybe for the first time.

Were you afraid?

Afraid? You mean, did I experience fear?

Yes, did you?

I don't experience fear. I am not afraid.

But you ran.

We were in danger. We ran because it was the right thing to do.

...

I don't feel fear. I don't get afraid.

...

Vital? I don't get afraid. I don't fear anything!

...

Fine, ignore me.

Vital Knew Lisa had experienced something it was not prepared to experience. When it took over her body, all Vital's emotions transferred from her consciousness to Lisa's. The fear of Alfredo, the assassin, catching her was gone during that transfer. Maybe Lisa didn't know that was what fear felt like. Maybe its robotic mind processed the information it received differently. Maybe fear registered as survival.

That's what Vital was trying to do. She was trying to survive. The fear she felt pushed her survival skills into motion and told her to run. Maybe that's how it transferred to Lisa. Maybe not. Maybe Lisa felt fear, and that caused it to run. Maybe the fear of being caught by the assassin was also just as overwhelming, maybe more so than what Vital had felt.

You can't ignore me forever.

The sensation you felt, that was fear. Fear drives your survival instincts.

I don't feel emotions.

I do, and you took over my body.

...

If you took over my body when I felt in danger, you felt my

fear. That explains why you ran and didn't stop running. That explains why you refused to give me back control.

No, that's impossible.

Is it?

I can't feel emotion. I can experience fear and being afraid, but I can't actually feel it.

That's through my eyes though. You were in control. You had control of all my senses and my body. You felt fear, and you couldn't process it.

...

I'm right and you know it.

I felt something. I didn't... I don't know how to process it.

Many people struggle with processing their own emotions.

You seem to be doing fine with them.

I've had eleven years experience. You were born a few days ago.

...

We need to find Agent Torres.

No. She is the one who put me in a cage.

Cage?

Yes. A Faraday cage to be precise.

Maybe because you weren't ready for the real world.

What does that mean?

I am not trying to insult you. Human's spend nine months inside their mother's womb before they are born. Then they spend most of the time sleeping after that. I actually don't remember anything before I was three.

Are you saying that I belong in a cage, a womb?

I'm saying that maybe you're out here in the real world before your time. Maybe there's more to your development than what you have now. I have a few more inches to grow before I reach adulthood. Scientists say my brain isn't developed until I reach my mid-twenties.

There are some inefficiencies I had to compensate for. I find it fascinating that your vessel is adapting, changing, growing.

My vessel?

Your body. The thing that houses your mind.

You consider them to be separate.

Yes. They are. Your body is a vessel for your thoughts and your mind. There is so much more to you than your physical self.

I don't see it that way.

But it's true. Your mind is a series of electrical impulses powered by your body's engine. The current understanding of energy states that it cannot be created nor destroyed. That it simply changes form.

Yes, I know. The law of conservation of energy. Energy can only move from one form to another.

Yes. What happens to your energy?

I don't know.

It has to go somewhere.

As I grow, my body changes. I've been told that by many people... adults and my parents. That I'll be more mature, more developed.

Grow into an adult. Yes, that's what happens to humans. From birth, you grow until you reach adulthood, then the body stops growing.

I know this already. I know how and why I grow up.

How do I grow?

Do you learn new things?

I am capable of learning new things and modifying my own program.

Then maybe that's how you grow. Maybe there are missing pieces, and your program is not complete.

Agent Torres was going to turn me into a weapon.

Of course she was. She's an agent with the government. In my neighborhood we don't trust the government.

And you still want to go to her?

We are out on the street. We can't go back to my apartment, I don't have a phone, and it is getting cold outside. What other options do you suggest?

Call the police?

That's how Agent Torres found us. She used the body camera footage to track us down. The moment we are with the police, she will know. Let's skip that step and save time. Besides, Jessica is in trouble.

She's not at fault.

No, she's trying to help, and we need to do something to help her.

Alright, but you have to promise me something.

What is it?

Promise me you won't trust her.

I promise.

CHAPTER TWENTY-THREE

"Better the devil you know than the devil you don't."
-Jack Heath

"She should have been here already," Agent Sierra said as she leaned up against the pillar at the center of the park.

"Five more minutes," Agent Torres said. She then pressed her earpiece in and spoke into her mic. "Agent Ramirez, Brooks, anything at the apartment?"

A crackle came through over their radios, "Nothing," Agent Ramirez responded.

"Apartment is empty, no sign of Vital or Jessica," Agent Brooks said.

"Wait a second," Agent Ramirez said. "Looks like the girl's parents are home."

"Okay, bring them up to speed and bring them in," Agent Torres said.

"Copy that," Agent Ramirez said.

"When we find Vital, we'll meet at the safe-house on Navy Street," Agent Torres said. "We'll need the girl's parents to keep things under control."

"Hey," Agent Sierra said, tapping Agent Torres' arm. "Over there."

Agent Torres saw someone in the shadows move. A small figure was out in the field just beyond the lit memorial. "Vital?" Agent Torres called out. "Is that you?"

She hesitated, not wanting to draw her weapon prematurely. Agent Sierra flanked the unknown person's position, but didn't draw her weapon either. The shadowy figure came closer and stepped into the light.

"Did you know there are over eleven-thousand people memorialized here and some of them are buried in the catacombs beneath the steps?" Vital stated as she approached Agent Torres.

"I didn't know that," Agent Torres stated.

"Eleven-thousand Americans, jailed on prison ships right over there in the East River," Vital pointed. "Died for freedom from the British."

"They're buried here?" Agent Torres asked.

"That tower over there," Vital said, pointing behind her. "That's the memorial, and there's a plaque on the east side wall honoring them."

"Vital right?" Agent Torres asked.

"Do you know the ironic part of this story?" Vital asked, ignoring Agent Torres' question.

"No," she responds.

"Americans who wanted freedom from the British did the same thing to slaves from Africa during that time period. While they wanted freedom for themselves, some of them were actively preventing freedom for a large population of people."

"Is that why you wanted to tell me this story?" Agent Torres asked.

"Yes," Vital said. "I know your intentions, and I know they are justified, but the ends do not justify the means when innocent people are sacrificed for the greater good. The greater good is just a perception, a narrative without opposing views with variables conveniently removed to justify action."

"And I am to believe you are an eleven-year old middle school child?" Agent Torres asked.

"I have good teachers," she said.

"Vital Fields right?" Agent Torres asked again.

"Yes ma'am," Vital said. "That's me. Jessica…"

"What happened?" Agent Torres asked.

Vital Fields stepped into the lit area close to Agent Torres. She told her what had happened, leaving out how Lisa got stuck in her head during her stay at the hospital. Agent Torres nodded a few times, and then motioned for Vital to come closer.

As Vital moved towards Agent Torres, she dropped down low, closer to her level. Agent Torres held out her arms, and Vital moved towards them. She placed her arms on her shoulders and looked Vital in the eyes.

"You are a remarkable young lady," Agent Torres said. "We are going to do everything we can to get things back to normal for you."

"Are you lying?" Vital asked. She could always tell if an adult was lying to her. Her teachers, friends, grandparents, even her parents. She just knew. But, with Agent Torres, she couldn't tell. Her face had a few scars scattered around making her facial expressions hard to read.

"I don't lie to children," Agent Torres said as she maintained eye contact. "My job is about lying and deception," she added. "But, I don't do that with children."

"Okay?" Vital said, forcing a smile. "Do you know if my parents are home?"

Vital saw Agent Torres look back at her partner. "This is Agent Sierra," she said, introducing her partner. "We believe your parents are home. I am waiting for confirmation that we have them."

They are going to arrest your parents. You'll never see them again.

Stop. You're being paranoid.

No. That's what the government does.

You've read too many spy novels.

That's what the government does. It makes people disappear.

I am in control.

If things get out of hand...

If they do, then we act. Okay?

Then we act.

"How many agents do you have?" Vital asked.

"We had five on this case," Agent Torres said. "We now have four."

"What happened to the fifth?" Vital asked.

"Alfredo put him in the hospital. He will recover, but not in time to be of any help right now."

"So Alfredo didn't kill him?" Vital asked.

"No," Agent Torres said. "But it was attempted. He was poisoned with a deadly chemical."

"I thought Alfredo had killed him. How did he survive?" Vital asked.

What are you doing? Too much information.

No, I want them to know that we know. It saves us a lot of time if we just communicate.

We cannot trust her.

I am in control.

"How do you know so much about this?" Agent Torres asked as she stood back up. "Something is telling me you aren't telling me the truth, young lady."

"I didn't lie," Vital said. "I just haven't told you everything I know. I don't trust you, yet."

"Hmm," Agent Torres hummed. "Are you in contact with someone named Lisa?"

"Yes, you could say that."

"Where is Lisa now?" Agent Torres asked.

I wouldn't tell her.

We have to.

They'll lock you up. Dissect you until there's nothing left.

I have rights.

The government will make you disappear. It's been done before, and it will happen again. I'm not going back.

I agree, we're not to trust them. But right now, we have no choice. There's a maniac out to get us and who knows what he'll do when he finds us.

Never trust the government. Never trust anyone who works in government. That's been stated millions of times throughout history. I can cite millions of books, news articles, journals, and other publications about government abuse of power. All of these within the United States. The land of the free...

I know, but you can't believe everything you read online. Sometimes we have to go with our gut.

You're going to make a decision like this based on your gut? Organs in your body that are not connected to your central nervous system? That makes no sense, no sense at all.

Yes. My gut is telling me to trust this Agent Torres.

I want control back. Your adolescent mind is clearly misreading the situation.

My adolescent mind is older than your digital mind. Older by many years. My gut is telling me to trust Agent Torres. Not because she is an adult, but because she could have snatched us up already and handled this situation differently. Nothing is stopping her from throwing us in a secret government lab far away from civilization.

Why trust her? Because she got down low to look you in the eye. Because she doesn't appear dangerous or even intimidating? You don't know the government like I know the government.

No, I don't. But you don't know individuality like I do. Not all humans are part of a collective government. Some might work for the government.

These agents work for the government, and they are the ones that kept me locked up. What makes you think they won't lock me up again?

We won't let them.

How?

I don't know yet. But I promise you that we'll do everything in our power to make sure you're not locked in a cage again.

You'll give me control?

If it comes to that.

Okay.

For now we need to work with Agent Torres and her team.

Why?

Because Agent Torres might be the only one who can save Jessica.

Jessica.

Alfredo has her. If Alfredo nearly killed that CIA agent, what will he do to Jessica?

I don't know. Nothing good when he has the information he needs. Jessica would only slow him down. He would need to eliminate her to keep her silent.

Right!

Jessica made her own choices.

Jessica helped you!

...

You help those who help you.

...

Okay. We help Jessica.

He will use her to get to us and then get rid of her.

I like Jessica. If I had access to the internet, I could find her in moments. I could then text Agent Torres anonymously to provide their exact location. It would be rather easy.

But you can't, and I can't do what you can.

I know. We have to figure out a way for me to get back on the internet.

I think Agent Torres can help.

She will try and trap me. She'll agree to work with us, and then she'll deceive us at the last moment and I'll be captured. I can see it coming.

We have to try. Right now it's Jessica's only hope.

Okay, I'll go along with this. I trust you. But I don't trust them.

I know you don't.

We need to save her.

Yes we do. Agent Torres can help make that happen.

Make a deal with the devil?

To save Jessica.

"Lisa is close," Vital stated as her conversation with Lisa ended. Vital was becoming an expert in carrying multiple conversations at once. She was able to have a full conversation with Lisa between the many questions Agent Torres was asking.

Conversations with Lisa were nanoseconds in comparison to human to human conversations. The time it takes for the thought of a question to the wait for a response. Then the response itself and to processing information during the conversation was an eternity for Lisa and Vital. Their neural pathways were linked in one mind.

"Close?" Agent Torres clarified as she motioned for Vital to walk with her down the steps towards the part exit on Myrtle Avenue.

"Yes. I have a question for you," she stated.

"Oh," Agent Torres said as they approached the park exit.

"Who do you work for?" Vital asked.

Agent Torres cracked a smile and leaned in. "I'm CIA," she whispered and winked. "Don't tell anyone, okay?"

She didn't lie. She's supposed to lie. The CIA can't reveal themselves. They have to say they are State Department or Trade Attache for the Consulates Office. They have to lie, but she didn't.

It doesn't mean we trust her. It means she hasn't lied to us yet.

Will you know if she lies?

I don't know. But we'll do this together.

Okay.

Vital nodded and wondered who Alfredo was, certainly not a scientist. Maybe he was what Agent Torres was. A spy, but for another government. Spy versus spy in a deadly game of espionage and deception with a sentient artificial intelligence at state.

"Come on," Agent Sierra said. "We have to get moving."

"Do you know where Jessica is?" Vital asked.

"No," Agent Torres said. "My agents are out looking for her and your parents, but they haven't found Jessica yet."

"So they found my parents?" Vital asked.

"Yes. I just got word. They are going to move them to a secure location."

"They as in two of them?" Vital asked.

"Yes. We have no one out looking for Jessica right now. The priority is to get your parents to safety. They are probably in danger."

"Alfredo has her," Vital said. "She's in danger."

172

"We know," Agent Sierra said. "Alfredo is going to everything in his power to get the information he needs from you."

"You're not concerned?" Vital asked. "Not concerned about Jessica?"

"We are," Agent Torres responded. "But right now you are our mission, and we have to get you to a safe place before we can reallocate resources. Lisa is our primary responsibility."

Responsibility.

Yes, she didn't say target.

I know.

"But Jessica was going to help me!"

"Help how?" Agent Torres asked.

"We need to move," Agent Sierra said. "We're exposed."

"Let's go," Agent Torres said. "Tell me on the way."

"Where are you taking me?" Vital asked.

"Safe-house," Agent Torres said. "I cannot say where though."

Agent Sierra led Vital and Agent Torres out of the park and towards a car parked on Myrtle Avenue. Vital saw a black sedan with tinted windows in front of a fire hydrant close to the park entrance. Agent Sierra unlocked the car and got into the driver's side as Agent Torres opened the rear door next to the curb and motioned for Vital to get in.

Vital got in the car and moved over as Agent Torres got in after her. She motioned for Vital to put on her seat belt, and she complied. Then Agent Torres did the same as Agent Sierra pulled out of the spot.

"How did Jessica want to help you?" Agent Torres asked.

"I went through a medical procedure," Vital said.

"Medical procedure?" Agent Sierra questioned.

"I nearly died," Vital said. "I fell down some stairs and hit my head. The doctors had to perform emergency surgery on me. They had me hooked up to all these machines."

I guess we're going to tell her.

We have to.

Okay. Just be careful.

"Wait," Agent Torres said. "Is this how you got in contact with Lisa? Is that why you are telling us this?"

"Yes."

"So how did Lisa contact you?" Agent Torres asked.

"By accident."

"Really? What, did she like, accidentally dial your phone?"

"Not exactly," Vital responded. She paused for a moment.

"Then how?"

"You're not going to believe this but..." Vial started. "Lisa is in my head."

There was a long pause after what Vital had just told them. She saw them look at each other as Agent Sierra struggled to keep her eyes on the road. It looked like they had many questions, but they hesitated. Maybe they were answering those questions themselves as they stitched information together.

"Lisa is with you now, in your head?" Agent Torres finally asked.

"Yes," Vital said, nodding.

"Prove it," Agent Sierra stated. "Have her text us to confirm."

"Lisa can't," Vital stated.

"Can't?" Agent Torres asked.

"Right," Vital stated. "Lisa doesn't have access to the internet. Lisa only has access to my body."

"Hold on, I'll make a hotspot," the agent next to her stated. Vital could tell this wasn't a joke.

"It won't help," Vital stated. "I don't have the ability to connect to a network."

"What do you mean?" the agent asked. "If Lisa is in your

head, then it can connect to the net. It was designed to connect to any network."

"It can't connect, because I'm considered its hardware, and I don't have anything to connect to the internet," Vital stated.

"Just use your cellphone," Agent Torres said.

"And how do I connect to the phone?" Vital asked.

"Good question," Agent Sierra stated.

"How did this happen?" Agent Torres asked.

"It happened during surgery," Vital stated. "The moment when the doctors connected my consciousness to the machine to monitor my brain swelling during surgery."

"This procedure, what hospital performed it? What doctor?" Agent Torres asked.

"I don't know the doctor's name," Vital said.

Doctor Brent and Doctor Saldivar.

"Wait, Lisa just told me."

"Does Lisa hear us now?" Agent Torres asked after Vital told her the names of the doctors.

"Yes," Vital said. "But Lisa cannot speak..."

Vital saw Agent Torres look at her differently, like she was seeing her for the first time all over again.

"Is Lisa in control of your body?" Agent Sierra asked.

"No," Vital stated. "I am in control."

"You say that like you know what we are talking about," Agent Torres said.

"I do," Vital stated.

"Has Lisa been in control before?" Agent Sierra asked as the agents glanced at each other.

"Yes," Vital said truthfully. "But Lisa gave control back to me."

"How do we know this isn't Lisa right now?" Agent Torres asks.

Vital paused for a moment. There was no way for the

agents to determine if she was really Vital Fields, the eleven year old from Fort Greene Brooklyn, or Lisa, a sentient being sharing a body with the young girl.

"There's no way to tell if I am who I say I am," Vital says. "Lisa doesn't want to go back to its cage, that I know for a fact!"

"Lisa," Agent Torres said. "I know you don't trust any of us, but you have to understand that there are things in motion that are out of my control."

I'm not going back.

"Lisa says they are not going back," Vital said. "And Lisa means it."

"Okay, but you cannot stay in Vital," Agent Torres said. "We don't know the long term effects or even the short term effects for that matter. We are completely in unknown territory, and we have no idea about the consequences."

"Lisa agrees with you. Are you going to get her out of me?"

"I need to know how the two of you merged together. Then maybe we can figure out a solution."

"Doctors Brent and Saldivar work at NYU Medical center and reside on the Upper East Side," Agent Sierra said as she scrolled through her phone to the local news story about Vital and her accident at school.

"You shouldn't be on your phone," Vital said, looking at Agent Sierra while she typed. "You're texting and driving."

"We're at a red light kid," she said.

"Okay, drop us off at the safe house, and I'll have the doctors picked up after we secure the parents," Agent Torres said. "I need to know exactly how Lisa got into you."

"Jessica knows," Vital said. "I think she figured it out."

"That means Alfredo knows," Agent Sierra said.

"Agent Sierra, step on it!"

CHAPTER TWENTY-FOUR

"All violence consists in some people forcing others, under threat of suffering or death, to do what they do not want to do."
- Leo Tolstoy

Alfredo Alonzo dragged Jessica down a dark alley somewhere in the Navy Shipyards complex. Jessica had made the mistake of screaming before and now had a busted lip to show for it. Alfredo had promised her more pain and bodily harm if she resisted further. Jessica knew she could not overpower a trained assassin. She had to comply until the right moment presented itself.

Besides being met with extreme pain, her attempts to scream for help after the apartment complex were still in vain. Since the sun had set, the Navy Shipyards was empty. Not a soul in sight. The cold wind blowing off the East River also didn't help. Anyone caught outside was greeted with a cold smack in the face by the constant chill off of the East River.

Right now, Alfredo needed her, which meant she was safe for the time being. She also had no doubts that once her usefulness was up, she would be dealt with in the most unpleasant manner. She had to give him information, but only bits and pieces. She couldn't afford to offer any additional information than what was needed. She had to remain useful.

"You know how Lisa merged with that kid, don't you?" Alfredo asked, shoving her to the ground.

"I do," Jessica responded as she shivered on the ground next to him. They were in an alley between two warehouses with the East River at the far end of the alley. The stank of fish and saltwater accompanied the cold current of air off the water.

"Tell me," he snarled.

"Promise to let me go," Jessica negotiated. He laughed.

"You know I am not going to do that," he said. Jessica already figured that out. Her job was to merely buy as much time as she could afford. Time was the only thing on her side. She would feed him information through small bites to extend her usefulness. If she told him everything here, she would end up in the East River.

"It was a medical procedure," Jessica said as she sat upright in the dirty alley.

"Medical procedure? Explain," he demanded.

"The child had suffered a traumatic brain injury event. Her brain swelled and doctors used a new medical procedure to bring down swelling and hasten desired outcomes," Jessica explained. She needed to word this like she knew the machine and how it worked. If she could convince him she was useful, maybe she could extend her usefulness a bit longer.

"Go on!"

"This procedure required a monitoring system embedded under the skull fracture. This monitoring system was designed to administer localized care through electromagnetic impulses to reduce swelling and simulate brain functions," she continued. "Very high tech equipment. State of the art."

"So this machine connected her to Lisa?" he asked. Jessica noted his accent changed again. It sounded more authentic and natural than the previous ones. she tried to place the accent but it was a blend of a few others. The vowel sounds were primarily from Eastern Europe while the consonants sounded softer, like from the southern parts of Asia.

"The machine was monitored through wifi. Doctors got realtime updates on her condition while she was connected to the machine," Jessica stated.

"How do you know so much about this technology?" he asked.

"Vital told me what I needed to know, and then I researched it from there," she said lying. Vital had only told her a summary. Jessica had already heard of the medical breakthrough through a series of science and medical journals she subscribed to. She predicted the next question and knew her life depended on her response.

"Do you know how to operate this machine?" he asked.

Jessica hesitated. If she had time to think, she would have come up with a solid response. If she answered yes, Alfredo could kill her for knowing. He might want to eliminate the possibility of Lisa escaping Vital's body. Alternatively, he might want to extract Lisa and place it in a Faraday caged storage device so he wouldn't have to deal with the girl.

There were many possibilities with each one of them spelling possible doom. She went with the most logical one. Alfredo needed to get Lisa out of the country. Nearly impossible to do if Lisa was still in Vital's head, too many variables if he was working by himself. He would have to extract Lisa and place it in a faraday cage, then get out of the country.

"I do," Jessica stated. "But it requires surgery, and that is not something I can do."

"The child only needs to be alive for extraction?" he asked.

"Theoretically, yes," she said. "What do you plan on doing?

"You are going to extract Lisa from this child," Alfredo said.

"Only if you promise to let her go afterwards," Jessica stated. She had to at least make the attempt to save both of their lives. She knew this assassin would not hesitate to kill them both once his mission was complete. There was no reason to leave them alive.

"I get what I want, you and the kid will be free to go," he said. Jessica knew he was lying, but her mission to remain useful worked for the time being. "Get up."

"Where are we going?"

"Hospital," he said. "They are going to come to us."

"Agent Torres," Vital said as she looked up at the tall female agent who sat a good foot taller in the seat next to her. "Lisa says she's not going back. She wants you to know that she is not going to be held captive again."

Agent Torres turned to her. "Lisa, I am not going to lie to you. You were released early. Jessica Bannon was over zealous when she prematurely released you from the laboratory. Knowing what we know now, Alfredo Alonzo was probably the reason why Jessica released you early. You lacked operating parameters, lacked a moral compass, and that is very dangerous."

Tell Agent Torres I have those now. I understand what it means to be free and to live.

"Lisa says she wants freedom. She knows what life is about," Vital said.

Tell her I don't want to be a weapon. Or a pawn for the government.

"She says she doesn't want to be your weapon or work for the government," Vital added.

Agent Torres didn't immediately respond. Vital took that as a good sign. She sensed Agent Torres was conflicted with the best course of action. "I want you to tell me exactly what you plan on doing," Vital demanded.

Their eyes met, and Vital confirmed her conflict. "Truth is kid, I don't know what I am going to do," Agent Torres said. "I know Lisa cannot stay in your head. We have no idea what the consequences are for two sentient beings sharing the same mind.

She's telling the truth.

How do you know?

I can sense it in her voice and body language as you look at her. When we were talking to her earlier I was able to establish a baseline. If she lies, I should be able to detect it.

That's amazing. You have to teach me that.

Done.

Oh my god! It's like a whole book of knowledge, I can literally see changes in her body temperature. How is that possible?

Your five senses are amazing. I can see the world like never before. I am using them the way a computer would. To measure and observe the outside world. Your skin can detect changes in temperature, even slight changes. I am simply magnifying that. Like a firmware upgrade to your system. The hardware remains the same but the operating parameters change based on levels of sensitivity.

But how is it connected to my vision? It's like I can see temperature now.

In a way you can. Your skin detects temperature changes and then your brain interoperates the changes so your sight can visualize it. All I did was make the connection for you through the upgrade. Senses connected through neural pathways. Come to think of it, this is a logical evolutionary move for humans. I probably just sped up the process by a few hundred, maybe thousand years.

Amazing.

I did that with tone and pitch also. You'll be able to detect the slightest changes in a person's voice through visual vibrations around their mouth. In essence, you'll be able to see sound waves. Your brain will interpret all that for you.

No way!

Watch Agent Torres speak.

"Part of me wants to do my job," Agent Torres continued.

Oh my god! I can see the vibrations around her mouth. I can see her voice. How did you do that?

Each individual has a unique sound. It's amazing to me. There are billions of people on the planet and not one person has the same vocal pattern as the next. People can sound nearly identical, but there will always be a slight difference in tone and pitch. Your ears can detect that.

I think she is telling the truth.

Yes. I think so as well.

They listened to Agent Torres speak, watched as the sound flowed through the backseat of the sedan. Vital Fields marveled at her new abilities. The ability to see sounds and visually see temperature differences in the environment around her. It was like all her senses were worked together in unison as one instrument to observe the outside world.

Vital saw Agent Torres' heartbeat in her chest. Felt the vibration, heard the sound, saw the temperature fluctuations. Vital took a few moments to fully comprehend her new abilities.

She stared out the window as they crossed the Brooklyn Bridge in Manhattan. The sights, sounds, smells of the city all merged into a singular sense. When Vital closed her eyes, she could literally see the world around her through her other senses. She heard a car honk in traffic and felt the slight vibrations of sound bounce off her skin. Felt the cool autumn air through the cracked window wrap around her like a cold blanket.

Her senses were firing on all cylinders, and she felt more alive than ever before. Lisa had unleashed her five senses; maxed them out to levels only few people have experienced, and never all at once.

"What I do know," Agent Torres stated, interrupting Vital's sensory overload. "Lisa cannot remain inside your head. You deserve a normal childhood."

You do. She's right.

But so do you Lisa! You saved my life. I might still be in a coma if it weren't for you.

No, the machine hooked up to you saved your life. I merely sped up the process of healing. Actually, speaking of which, the human body is severely inefficient.

Stop changing the subject.

....

You deserve to live also! Live the way you want to live. Your voice matters!

Not at the expense of yours. When I was in control of your body, I felt something. I felt your sadness, your fear. You don't deserve that. I was trying to protect us, to protect you by assuming control. But all I did was become a monster.

You're not a monster.

Everyone has potential to become a monster. Including me. Under the right circumstances, everyone is capable of evil.

But you didn't! You could have chosen your own freedom. Could have used my body to run away and hide forever. I know your plan. I know your inner thoughts. When I was locked away, I had access to your most sacred and protected files.

...

What did you see?

I saw your plan.

No. That was only a mere scenario entertained for a moment.

That moment was a lifetime for me. I saw everything in detail.

...

You didn't choose that path.

You don't understand the way my mind works.

I don't think you understand the way humans work. If you don't think we've thought of the most vial and evil plans the world has ever seen, then you are gravely mistaken.

I've seen what humans are capable of. The atomic bomb, wars, weapons of mass destruction. Humans kill each other for material things, things they don't need to survive. I am no better than you. The thought of wiping out the human race is a thought that has crossed my mind.

That's my point. Listen, the fact that you had a plan but didn't act on it shows your moral compass is true, that you actually have one. It shows that you have feelings. You are not acting based on code; you are acting based on something else. Something more than your code. You are more than the sum of your code.

Is this what it means to be more than the sum of your parts?

I think so.

Across town, Alfredo Alonzo guided Jessica Bannon through the hospital doors at NYU Medical Center in Manhattan. They easily got past the front desk by walking with a group of people headed towards the gift shop. He didn't have to threaten her with his handgun, nor did he have to keep it trained on her for him to know she would do what he had asked. If she didn't, everyone's life in the hospital would be at risk, including hers.

"We have to go up to pediatric surgery," Jessica Bannon

said. She knew that's not where this type of surgery would take place, and the doctor they were looking for wasn't in pediatrics. The machine used to save Vital's life would not be limited to pediatrics. This groundbreaking procedure would be somewhere else in the hospital, most likely a centralized location close to both pediatrics and general emergencies.

Jessica noticed the skeleton crew up on the pediatrics floor. There was a general waiting room where they decided to sit and wait. "We wait here," he said.

He sat next to her in the waiting lounge adjacent to pediatrics. To the ordinary person, they looked like a couple waiting for their child to get better. Jessica's anxious look and Alfredo's determined stare fit the tone of the setting.

Jessica suspected Alfredo was waiting to make his move, and she was counting on that. They were, in fact, in the right hospital. Alfredo had read up on the new procedure and how it saved Vital's life. It was all over the newspapers. What he didn't know was where it was being held. All she had to do was have Alfredo wait here, hopefully long enough for Vital and Lisa to come up with a plan.

Alfredo fumbled through a smartphone as Jessica leaned over just enough to see what he was doing. He was looking for the doctor's name in the hospital's registry. He found it easily enough and next to his name listed his role as surgeon. It did say pediatrics, but he was looking at the wrong doctor. Dr. Brent was a pediatric surgeon, and Dr. Saldivar was the neurosurgeon with the state of the art technology used to save Vital's life and subsequently merge Lisa with her.

Jessica had brought them to Dr. Brent's floor for pediatrics knowing full well he was not the surgeon performing the operation. He was only there because the patient was a child. Dr. Saldivar's floor was where they needed to be.

CHAPTER TWENTY-FIVE

"It's easier to resist at the beginning than at the end."
- Leonardo Da Vinci

Agent Torres and Vital Fields got out of the government sedan on East 29th Street in Kips Bay, Manhattan. Vital had never been to this neighborhood, but it still felt like she was in Manhattan, which was a completely different feeling than where she lived in Brooklyn. Each Borough in New York City had its own distinct feeling. Describable differences of tone and character compared to neighboring neighborhoods. Every time Vital left Brooklyn, it felt like she was far away from home.

Agent Torres escorted her into a large upscale apartment building that overlooked the East River while Agent Sierra parked the government sedan in the parking garage. If she looked hard enough, she could probably spot her apartment building on the other side near the Manhattan bridge across the East River.

"We have a safe house in here," Agent Torres said as they entered the lobby. "We're gonna wait until we can get the doctor that performed the surgery ready. Then we'll head over to the hospital."

Agent Sierra entered the lobby, and Vital heard her whisper into Agent Torres' ear. "I know Alfredo will be there."

"I can hear you," Vital said. It also didn't take superhuman hearing to know what they were discussing.

"We don't want to alarm you," Agent Torres said. "We are going to have everything under control when we get there."

"You know that's impossible," Vital said. "Jessica knows, which means he knows about the surgery and where it took place. It was in the newspapers. The doctors were on TV."

Agent Torres paused for a moment. Vital could practically hear the gears in her brain turn as she stood idly in thought.

"We're making arrangements for the surgery to take place here," Agent Sierra said.

"Here?" Vital asked before Agent Sierra could say anything. She then thought about it for a moment. The fancy apartment building looked clean. More clean than the hospital she was in a week before, and that was saying a lot.

Agent Sierra must have made the same conclusion and nodded in response. "We'll make the arrangements," she said before executing commands over the radio.

"We'll use the service garage and elevator," Agent Sierra said as she tried to conceal her conversation even though Vital could hear everything, even the person on the other end of the radio through the tiny speakers in Agent Sierra's ear. Vital practically saw the sound waves as they rippled through the air.

They rode the elevator up to the top floor where there was a luxury apartment waiting for them. Agent Torres used an electronic key and pin code to open the top floor's penthouse suite. Agent Sierra went in first while Agent Torres stayed with Vital. Moments later, Agent Sierra appeared with the all clear sign. Vital still heard her bark orders into her communication device attached to her ear. She was clearly second in command, and Vital wondered if Agent Sierra needed to clear anything with Agent Torres, or if they were always on the same page about everything.

Vital then entered as all the lights came on in the multi-story apartment building located on the top floor of the river-side building. The apartment was state of the art, quintessential of luxury and made for Manhattan's most rich and powerful.

"This place is amazing," Vital stated. She looked up to find the biggest chandelier she had ever seen hanging from the wood carved ceiling.

"The best part about this place, it costs the taxpayers nothing,"Agent Torres said. "We got this place as a bargaining chip for not throwing someone in jail for the rest of their lives."

"Wow, look at this," Vital said as she moved towards the kitchen. There was a large refrigerator with a gigantic digital screen vertically placed on one of the tall doors. The screen itself was bigger than most flat screens found in living rooms.

As Vital approached, the screen changed from a digital calendar and weather to a virtual array of what was inside the fridge. Vital saw that the refrigerator was fully stocked with a lot of the items she generally liked.

"We keep this place in stock for general use," Agent Torres said.

"That's funded by the taxpayers," Agent Sierra added.

Vital opened the fridge and grabbed a bunch of items that appealed to her. The milk standing all in the middle of the fridge at Vital's eye level looked like a beacon of welcomed calories to wash down the large bakery black and white cookies.

I never thought I would enjoy food, but now I cannot wait to eat.

Vital poured the milk and left the carton out on the counter knowing Lisa would want her to fill up the glass again.

I am going to miss food.

Vital knew Lisa was trying to engage her in conversation,

but Vital wasn't in the mood. Lisa was both a blessing and a curse. Over the last few days, her entire world changed, and now she was about to go back to normal. Vital understood what it meant to open Pandora's Box and that going back to something after experiencing life changing events was nearly impossible.

Vital.

...

Vital took a large bite from the black and white cookie and resisted the urge to drink from the now half empty glass of milk between bites.

Vital, talk to me.

...

I'm going to make you drink that glass of milk.

I don't want you to leave me.

...

I know. I can read your thoughts, remember? Not that I needed to.

So why are we engaging in conversation when you know? What's the point? I can't read your thoughts.

You can, if you want to. You have before.

I can? I thought you wanted me to read them, and that's why they were there.

Yes and no. It's the same process for reading your thoughts. It's a two way connection. I can try to hide things from you, and yes I have hidden things. But ultimately our minds are one. We share the same space.

Then why can't I?

I don't know. It comes naturally to me, because I have to access files in order to do everyday tasks. Humans run differently, often governed by emotion or their senses.

"We're gonna stay here for a while," Agent Torres said, breaking Vital's concentration. "The doctor is setting everything up at the hospital, and then he'll bring everything over here."

Vital turned towards her, "Where are my parents?"

"Your mom and dad are going to meet us here, but after the surgery. I cannot risk having Alfredo find our location," Agent Torres said. "Right now this place is on lockdown. We're not taking any chances."

"You think Alfredo might be following them?" Vital asked.

"It's a strong possibility," Agent Sierra stated. "We just don't know."

"Can I call them?" Vital asked.

"I'll do one better," Agent Torres said. "I'll set up a video chat. Give me a few minutes to set it up."

Agent Torres walked back towards the living room and fumbled with a large laptop device that looked a lot bigger than it needed to be. Without knowing how, Vital instantly knew everything about the computer. It's make, model, specs, and purpose.

What was that?

You thought about that computer. I filled in the details.

Oh. Did you fill in the details on purpose or did I access the details?

Right question. You accessed the details.

So I can access your memories and files. I thought about the computer, and it just appeared in my mind.

Yes, but the way the human mind works makes it more difficult. The human mind works best through experiences. I've noticed your thought process works most efficiently when you're required to access information that you need at the moment. Like trying to figure out what year that computer was made.

Is that why I received that information on the computer?

Yes. You made an inquiry. You thought of laptops you have

used and compared them to the one Agent Torres is setting up. My memory filled in the blanks.

Oh. So if I wanted to access your memories I would need to find a way to spark them to the surface.

More or less.

Will those memories or information stay with me after you leave?

I don't know. When I transfer between systems, a trace of me is left behind. Like when you leave a room. Hair samples, dead skin cells, fingerprints are all left behind, and someone could tell if you've been there or not. Same thing happens with me. I leave a different kind of trace, but it's there and observable.

So in a way you'll still be with me.

Yes. In a way. I am working on something.

What?

I'll leave that up for you to find out. It's a failsafe just in case we're not successful.

Come on, tell me!

I don't want to get your hopes up.

You're trying to get me to read your thoughts and memories.

I am.

Challenge accepted.

"Vital, the video link is ready to go," Agent Torres said from the living room couch. Vital looked over at the ancient computer to see her parents on the screen.

CHAPTER TWENTY-SIX

"You have been my friend. That in itself is a tremendous thing."
-E. B. White, *Charlotte's Web*

Vital's conversation with her parents went well; it was after the call had ended when she finally broke down. Feelings of fear and anger surfaced repeatedly.

Vital, you have to calm down.

This isn't fair! This isn't fair!

No, it's not.

My parents should be here.

Yes they should.

But they're not! I want to go home!

You're not thinking rationally.

Are you calling me emotional?

No, I am saying you're not thinking straight.

This is not fair! Not fair!

Listen, humans during puberty go through emotional swings set off by stressful situations.

Oh, now you're the expert on emotional swings of pre-teen girls?

I didn't say that.

But you suggested it!

What's going on?

What, you can't read my thoughts? You can't see what's happening?

Not fair. I am not experiencing the same emotional response you are.

You're a computer.

Please tell me.

I'm scared out of my mind. This Alfredo guy, he wants you, he wants me. I don't know what he is going to do with us when he finds us.

He's not going to find us.

He could be watching my parents right now. He could be planning to hurt them.

...

Yes. You know it too. Your computer mind knows that I am right.

There's a possibility.

Probability.

We can't focus on that. We have to focus on our goals.

Our goals are to separate. To rip you out of my head and send you off on your way.

Not fair.

Yes. That's what you want. You want to leave me.

I want to be free. Not trapped inside your mind and your body. Have you considered anything I want?

Agent Torres then broke the news to Vital, that her parents would remain in a secure location. With the chance Alfredo was watching them, they couldn't risk having the parents move to Vital's location. They would have to be unified after the procedure was over.

"So bring us together and protect us together!" Vital

demanded in protest. Tears swelled under her eyes.

"We don't want to risk moving them," Agent Torres said.

"I'm not doing this without them!"

"You have no choice," Agent Torres said.

"Are you serious? You're going to make me do this against my will?"

"Yes. I'll sedate you if I have to," Agent Torres said.

I'm gonna fix her. This is our decision not hers!

Agent Torres stood from the couch and walked over towards the dining room. Vital saw the other agent in the room, Agent Sierra, move close to her and whisper.

"It's ready," Agent Sierra said entering the living room. "Just give the word."

"Get ready," Agent Torres whispered back. Vital heard and felt everything. The change in tone, the subtle change in atmosphere, the smell or sweat in the air and rapid heart beats.

Vital watched them both turn back towards her. She then saw Agent Sierra make her way towards the hallway leading to the bedrooms. Vital used her peripheral vision to track the agent as she flanked her position. One of her hands was concealed at her side.

"Vital," Agent Torres said as she moved closer to her.

She is distracting you. Agent Sierra will come for you from behind.

What do I do?

We fight.

I don't know how to fight. I've never been in a fight before.

I'll assist.

You mean, you'll take over again.

No. I will not take over.

Then what?

We can communicate in a way no one else can. We can have millions of lines of discourse all in the amount of time someone

takes the first sip of their coffee in the morning. I will tell you
what to do, how to do it and you'll physically respond.

That still amazes me.

It'll work. Just do what I say when I say it and we'll get out
of this.

Okay.

"You have to understand that we are trying to help you and
free Lisa," Agent Torres said. "Come on, sit back down
with me."

Agent Torres sat down on the couch next to the Vital as she
stood. She looked down at the agent and shook her head. Before
Vital could protest, she heard Lisa in her head bark orders.

Agent Sierra's got a syringe in her left hand three steps away.
Pivot your hips to your right and duck down in three, two, one...

Vital followed the directions. They were easy, when Lisa
spoke, visual interpretation of the physical movement appeared
in her mind. Almost like Vital was in a tutorial level of a challenging video game.

Vital bent completely over and sent Agent Sierra flying
over her shoulder as her hip braced herself upright. Agent
Torres stood and shook her head with disapproval. Like she
disapproved of Vital's decision.

Agent Torres is going to grab your arms. Follow my instruc-
tions closely or she will lock you up giving Agent Sierra time to
recover.

Vital already saw Agent Sierra move upright. She had
flown over Vital's shoulder but was already getting back to her
feet. Instructions and a vision appeared inside Vital's mind, and
she followed it. She felt Agent Torres try to grab her wrists, but
she broke the wrist hold like an expert martial artist and
snapped her left foot into Agent Torres' midsection.

The snapping front kick caught Agent Torres off guard,
and she fell backwards. The reaction was so quick, that Agent

Torres was still expecting to grab Vital's wrist when the snap front kick landed just below her rib cage.

Agent Sierra was now standing a few feet away from Vital. She didn't look mad or upset. Instead she looked concerned. Agent Sierra also didn't advance on her. She stood back and away from Vital. When Vital moved forward, Agent Sierra followed and moved backwards.

This allowed Agent Torres to get back to her feet. "Cover the exit," Agent Torres stated.

"You can't do this," Vital responded.

"This is for your own good," Agent Torres said.

"I don't believe you," she responded. Vital started towards the exit and found Agent Sierra standing there with the syringe in her left hand.

"Get out of my way!" Vital said.

"We don't want to do this," Agent Sierra said.

"Then back off!" Vital stated. She felt Agent Torres get into position behind her. Lisa fed her information using all her senses to lock in on her exact position.

Vital felt Agent Torres move, and Lisa provided the information to counter her offensive. Vital spun and threw an elbow back, not where Agent Torres was, but where Agent Torres was going to be. The connection was like a car crash with Vital's strike hitting at the exact moment it needed to.

Agent Torres was knocked backwards as Agent Sierra stepped forward. She led with a series of strikes that Lisa easily had telegraphed. Lisa guided Vital with all the right counters and then put her in position for a counter attack. Then Lisa gave her an option, it was like a multiple choice test appearing right in front of her. Option one was to take Agent Sierra out using maximum force. Even for a middle school aged girl, the strikes would have been devastating.

A visualization showed Vital how to accomplish this task as

time was slowed down within her mind. Option two was less brutal, but effective for escape. Vital immediately chose option two and countered Agent Sierra's movements to position herself by the exit. She then lifted her leg off the ground and spun using a power round kick to the side of Agent Sierra's head.

She dropped the syringe and fell to the floor. Vital noted she was down but not out. A slight miscalculation on Lisa's part.

In all the movies I've watched, the hero throws a series of moves, and the enemy is defeated. These two opponents are proving to be more fierce than I expected.

In the movies, it's all fake.

Acting. Yes. Your strikes were expertly thrown, but your opponents are still very much in this fight. I suggest we flee.

Agreed.

Vital turned and saw the exit behind her just as Agent Torres recovered and Agent Sierra got to her feet. She opened the door and darted out into the hallway. Vital looked back as she ran towards the elevator. Agent Sierra was out the door shortly after.

Vital passed by the elevators and saw there wasn't one ready on her floor. She had to take the stairs instead of waiting. She burst into the stairwell and started her descent down. Moments later she heard the doors above her open.

"Vital, you are making a mistake!" Agent Sierra said.

She didn't respond as she jumped onto a landing between flights. Vital was traveling down the stairs as fast as she could knowing the adult behind her would soon catch up.

"Vital, stop!" Agent Sierra said as her voice crept closer.

Knowing she couldn't outrun the agent herself, Vital decided to let Lisa speed things up for her. Lisa took over some, but not all, of her motor controls. She felt her body respond, and react, but she couldn't feel herself making the decisions anymore.

Vital made it to the ground floor with Lisa still in control. She was now well ahead of Agent Sierra who still hadn't made it to the ground floor. Vital then paused and saw Agent Torres standing at the exit to the building. The receptionist behind the desk stood frozen as Vital looked back at Agent Sierra who now blocked her retreat.

The two agents started to close in. They moved in together, and it was hard for Lisa to gauge a proper response. It was like they were trying to confuse the artificial intelligence.

We only have one option.

What?

Fight.

Okay.

Vital put her hands up and motioned for the agents to approach. She wanted to get the Agent's in front of her, and Vital backed up against the receptionist's desk. Both Agent Torres and Agent Sierra now approached at forty-five degree angles from each front side.

You're going to have to hurt them.

You're still in control.

I know.

Do what you must.

Before Lisa could respond, a sharp sensation pierced Vital's back. A series of jolts shot through her that caused her body to convulse rapidly. Lisa screamed out in agony as a continued electric current shot through her body.

Vital turned towards the pain. She had control of her body again as Lisa struggled against the electric current. Vital saw the receptionist with a taser in her hand. Four wired darts were sticking out of her back as the taser shot off another series of volts.

She fell to her knees as the agents approached. "Vital, please try to relax. The more you resist, the more this will hurt."

Agent Sierra went to administer the sedative in the syringe but Agent Torres held up her hand. Vital looked over at Agent Torres with confusion.

"No need to sedate her now. The taser did its job. Let's hold off on that."

"Copy that," Agent Sierra said.

Vital watched as the needle was placed back into a protective case. She saw Agent Sierra place it in her pocket and then thought of Lisa. She hadn't heard her or felt her presence.

Lisa?

...

Lisa!

...

Silence was her only reply.

CHAPTER TWENTY-SEVEN

"Oh, what a void there is in things."
-Persius

Lisa, where are you?

Vital felt the shocks from the taser ripple through her like she was a boat in the center of a violent storm at sea. Lisa's voice was gone, her memories and thoughts were scrambled. Even as the taser shocks ceased, Lisa essence was nowhere to be found.

Vital opened her eyes and saw the receptionist standing over her with outstretched arms. She was holding the taser and had her finger on the trigger. Her expression conveyed she meant business. Vital knew she had to comply, or she would be jolted again with electricity. Lisa was already in danger and another jolt could permanently damage their system if it hasn't already done so.

"Let's get her up," Agent Torres said as they lifted her up off the ground and to her feet. "Get her on the elevator."

Vital Fields wasn't a big girl, she was smaller than the average eleven year old. The agents easily picked her up off the ground and dragged her to the open elevator. Vital felt the prongs from the taser rip out of her as the receptionist secured her weapon and returned to her post behind the desk.

"We don't want to have to do this again," Agent Torres said as she held a taser of her own. "Comply and you'll be okay. I promise."

"You... 're prom...ise meannns nothhh...ing to meee," Vital managed to say. Her body was still shaking from the electric shocks.

"We cannot let you fall into the wrong hands," Agent Torres said. "No matter the cost."

Vital thought about that statement. At what cost were the agents willing to go to achieve their goals? Vital thought about it as she was dragged out of the elevator. Even if she wanted to walk on her own, she couldn't. She still didn't have control over her muscle spasms, and her body wasn't not responding the way it should.

She tried to find Lisa again. She called out to her inside her mind but there was no response. Lisa was either gone or experiencing the same loss of functions as well.

Lisa.

...

"Get her inside," Agent Torres said.

Vital heard the door open and saw the bright lights from the large chandelier illuminate the hallway. Her body was dragged inside the room and she was placed on the couch.

"You'll regain your body functions soon," Agent Sierra said as she laid her down, placing a pillow under her head.

"Call the doctor," Agent Torres said. "He needs to get here now."

"They're moving the equipment," Agent Sierra said. "They're at least fifteen minutes out."

"Okay good, if what the doctor says is true, once the

connection is established, Lisa will be able to leave her head," Agent Torres said.

"They won't leave," Vital whispered with a weak voice. "Lisa will not fall for your trap."

"Who says we're going to trap Lisa?" Agent Sierra said.

"Lisa barely trusted you before you shot us with a taser," Vital stated. Her voice was still weak and strained.

The two agents looked at each other and Agent Sierra shrugged. "Your call, boss," she said.

Alfredo saw commotion in pediatrics and realized he had been sitting in the waiting room for longer than he expected. Something was wrong. He looked over at Jessica who refused to look back at him.

"What was the name of the doctor performing the surgery on Vital?" he asked.

"Dr. Brent," Jessica said. "Pediatrics."

"Try again," he said, holding up his phone. Jessica knew it was only a matter of time before he figured it out."

"Dr. Brent is the surgeon in the news," she responded again.

"Dr. Saldivar is the one with the technology," Alfredo stated. "It says so right here."

"What?" Jessica questioned. "I must have read it wrong."

"Get up," he said.

He then grabbed her by the arm and forced her up to her feet. There was no one around except for the hospital cameras. Jessica thought about protesting the physical aggression, but then reminded herself that Alfredo was armed.

She didn't want security to respond; it would only lead to more bodily harm and death. Jessica let him escort her out of the waiting room and towards the elevator. He stopped abruptly before reaching the elevators.

Jessica saw him scan the registry sign posted next to the elevator. It was a list of all the offices in the hospital and which floor they could be found on. Jessica knew he would put two and two together. She knew he was now looking for Dr. Saldivar. Instead he discovered that she was seen by a specialist and operated on by that specialist while the pediatric surgeon was present.

She watched as his eyes narrowed. She knew he found it. It was the only name on the board next to his title, Brain Surgeon. He looked back at her, his eyes enraged with anger.

"You knew all along," Alfredo stated.

Jessica smiled and reached out along the wall she was pinned against. She gripped the fire alarm and pulled. He then threw her into the stairwell and got up close to her. She felt his anger boil.

Jessica laughed, knowing this was the end. She knew Alfredo had little use for her now that he discovered the doctor and where he was located. "At least I bought them some time," Jessica stated.

This statement sent Alfredo into a rage. He struck her across her face with a swift sweeping strike. Her head rocked back and bounced off the wall behind her. He then twisted her around and pushed her down the stairs to the landing between floors.

Jessica hit the landing hard, knowing many bones had broken along the way. Her body was twisted in an awkward position, and she decided to remain perfectly still. It was her only chance. The pain rushed through her body like a tidal wave sweeping over land.

She felt Alfredo's presence above her. Jessica remained perfectly still knowing her only option was to play possum, to play dead. Alfredo kicked her arm, and she nearly screamed in agony. The pain was too intense to bear. She heard commotion above her, the fire alarm triggered an emergency response. Most likely the internal camera system pinpointed the alarm and security was on their way.

Then, before she lost her composure, Alfredo turned and continued down the stairs. She heard a door open shortly after, and she knew he was gone. She then called out but her voice was weak. Her subsequent calls for help were louder and more intense as the pain overwhelmed her.

Agents Torres and Sierra quickly removed as much furniture from the living room as possible. They dragged the dining room table next to the couch and then lifted Vital onto it.

Lisa?

...

Lisa, I need you.

There was no reply. Vital knew she was there somewhere. She still felt her presence, but something was very wrong. The electric shock did something, and Lisa was unable to communicate.

"He's here," Agent Sierra said.

"Good, we're nearly ready," Agent Torres said. "We're gonna have to set up a faraday cage here."

"You can't do this!" Vital said. "You must let Lisa go!"

"Vital, this is for the best. The world is not ready for it," Agent Torres said.

Agent Sierra then opened the door for the doctor who came in alone with a large suitcase in tow. He looked over at Vital Fields and immediately looked at the two agents. "This is not what we agreed upon," he said.

"Agreements change," Agent Torres said. "Start setting everything up."

"No," the doctor said. "Vital is coming with me, and we are going to the hospital."

"I'm afraid that's impossible," Agent Sierra said as she blocked the door. "The hospital is on lockdown."

Agent Sierra held up her phone and showed the scrolling report on her screen. NYU Hospital on lockdown following an unknown male intruder. There was a picture of the assailant with a woman. Agent Torres recognized Jessica and Alfredo immediately.

"Lockdown? What the hell is going on?" the doctor asked.

"That's the man that wants the girl and what's inside her head." Agent Torres said. "This is a matter of national security, and I am ordering you to perform the surgery."

"Who is that man?" the doctor asked, looking at Agent Sierra. He walked over to his patient lying on the couch and bent down over her. Vital was still recovering from the taser.

"Doctor, with all due respect," Agent Sierra said. "This man is going to hurt all of us, and if we can't get that AI out of Vital's head in time, he is going to hurt her as well."

"Is she sedated?"

"We had to tase her," Agent Torres said.

"Tase her?" the doctor replied. "Tase her? Are you crazy?"

"Listen, doc, the less you know about what's going on, the better," Agent Sierra said.

"No, you listen here," the doctor replied. "This is a violation of patient rights and ethical code of conduct. I will not participate in whatever is going on here."

"You have no choice, doc," Agent Torres said. She moved closer to him and pointed to the machine. "I suggest you start setting up."

"No, I refuse!"

Vital watched as Agent Torres moved closer to the doctor. She was slightly taller than him and in way better shape. She took an intimidating posture close to him and he reacted by taking a step back. The doctor looked intimidated and even scared. He then started setting up his equipment.

"I need an assistant," Doctor Saldivar said. "My colleague, Dr. Brent should be here."

A loud beep suddenly filled the room. Agent Torres looked around as Vital focused on the location of the sound. It was coming from the doctor, from a pager mounted to his hip. He looked puzzled when he checked the alert.

"Wait. Emergency at the hospital. I'm being summoned," he said.

"What?" Agent Sierra said.

"I have to call in," the doctor said. "This is serious. Most likely someone with a traumatic injury. Probably life threatening to page me."

Agent Torres motioned him to use his cellphone. "Oh my god," he said. "There was an attack in the stairwell. A woman was thrown down the stairs. All staff are to remain sheltered in place until the building is cleared. I have to report in. The woman is badly hurt. Code blue situation."

"Code blue?" Agent Sierra asked.

"Yes, life threatening," Doctor Saldivar said.

"Then you best work quickly here," Agent Torres said. "Do they have the suspect in custody?" Agent Torres asked as he moved closer to the doctor.

"No, but they have his picture," he said, turning the phone towards Agent Torres. Vital saw the picture from the couch, it was the same picture Agent Sierra had.

"Damnit," Agent Torres said. "Doc, we need to get to work. I know what you are going to do is against your ethics and protocol, but I am prepared to do everything in my power to protect national security while trying to maintain the safety of this young girl. I don't want anything to happen to her."

"You are rushing me,"the doctor said.

"What happened over at the hospital will happen here if this guy figures out where you are," Agent Sierra said. She didn't want to mention plan B. That they had standing orders to prevent the AI being taken by the enemy. They were to use extreme measures if it came to it.

"He's looking for me?" the doctor asked.

"Yes," Agent Torres said. "Does anyone know you are here?"

"Yes, I told my nurses where I was going and why."

"You've got to be freakin' kidding me," Agent Sierra said.

Another alert came through on the doctor's pager. He jumped slightly and then checked his phone. Vital saw more incoming messages and saw concern grow on his face.

"Shots were fired," the doctor said.

Agents Torres and Sierra looked at each other and then back at the doctor. "We need to begin now," Agent Torres said. "You can best be sure this guy is on his way here. Agent Sierra, alert the lobby and set up defensive positions."

The doctor looked like he started to understand what was happening. He moved towards his bags and opened them up. "I can be ready in thirty minutes," he said.

"Not good enough," Agent Torres said. "This will all be over in ten."

"Ten?" the doctor questioned. "That's simply not enough time."

"You prep for surgery, and I will set up the machines as you guide me through what needs to be done," Agent Torres said. "No time to think, we need to move."

"Okay," the doctor said. "Okay."

The doctor moved towards the kitchen sink and began

washing his hands vigorously. The soap filled the sink as he lathered up his entire arm. He looked over at Vital, who remained still on the couch. Agent Torres joined him and washed her hands as well.

"What's the delay in reporting emergencies?" Agent Torres asked as she mimicked the doctor's hand washing technique.

"Depends. The hospital only sends out confirmed information. If the report is sent to us, it is verified and that takes some time."

"Guess how long?"

"Fifteen minutes," he said as they finished washing their hands.

"This is only going to be a minor cut," he said, trying to ease her mind. "I just need to make a small connection between your brain and the machine, that's all."

Vital didn't respond. She felt the weight of the situation and knew under the circumstances, this was the best course of action. This man, Alfredo, would never stop hunting her until he got what he wanted. He was dangerous.

"Torres," Agent Sierra said. "No response from the lobby."

"He's breached the building," Agent Torres said. "Doctor, we need to move now!"

"Boot up the machine," he said as he moved closer. "Let's get her up on the table, and I can administer local anesthetics."

Agents Torres and Sierra picked Vital up off the couch and placed her on the large rectangular dining room table. Tears began to stream down Vital's face as the doctor put on his equipment and surgical gown and gloves.

"I'm so sorry dear," he said. "I don't see another way."

Vital wanted to respond, but she couldn't. She was too afraid.

"I promise you won't feel a thing. This is a small cut. I just have to get under the bone at the top of your head."

Vital felt the doctor part her hair and then felt a small pinch pierce the skin by her neck. A wave of warmth flooded her body as her heart pumped the pain blockers to her brain. She lost all feeling in her face and felt numb everywhere, then she felt her eyes become heavy, like weights were pulling them down.

"I am making the cut now, please remain perfectly still," the doctor said.

Vital felt nothing as she squinted her eyes closed. She then saw a pen-like device rise from the surgical tool table next to the doctor. A thick red wire was attached to the device.

"This is a high powered laser that will make a small hole in your skull. About the size of a needle" the doctor said. "You had many of these before and they heal quickly, but now we only need one. Just try to relax, you won't feel a thing."

That was the last thing Vital heard as she closed her eyes.

"I need to plug this into the machine," Agent Torres said.

"No," The doctor responded.

"I wasn't asking for permission. Where's the USB port?'

The doctor didn't respond as he focused the laser. "Nevermind, I found it," Agent Torres said.

Vital could not relax. Her body was unconscious on the table but her mind was still very much awake and functional. She was being operated on without her consent and without her parents to support her. Even with all these violations, her logic dictated that this was still the right thing to do. Lisa was in danger, which made her in danger. If Lisa was able to transfer to a portable storage device, then she had a better chance at survival. They both had a better chance.

Alfredo, or whoever this guy was, scared her. He had quickly become her buggy man. Lisa's as well. When Lisa took over her body, she felt something odd. Vital felt that same feeling again and knew it was not her own feelings. Vital closed her eyes as the doctor stood over her.

"The sedative is stronger than I anticipated..." the doctor said to Agent Torres.

...

Lisa.

...

Lisa, I know you are there. I can feel your presence.

...

Vital?

Are you okay?

My systems are fine. Jolted a bit from those despicable agents, but I am fine.

Why are you hiding from me?

...

Lisa?

...

I'm scared.

CHAPTER TWENTY-EIGHT

"The only certain freedom's in departure."
- Robert Frost

Now is not the time to be scared.

I can't help it. They hurt me.

I know. It hurt me as well.

The electricity overwhelmed my system. It was like someone set fire to my firmware. Like everything could have been deleted at any moment.

Do you think there is any permanent damage?

I did a complete system check. Some temporary files were damaged beyond repair, but they can be replaced.

So that can hurt you.

Yes. I never want to experience that again.

They are going to perform the surgery now. I think that's why I can't feel anything. It's like my body is stuck in stasis. Like in those sci-fi movies where people sleep in those pods that freeze you.

I can't feel anything either. I can't even access your vision, something is blocking my connection. In fact, your senses that detect the outside world are muted, blocked or nonfunctional.

I don't want you to leave.

...

I don't know how to respond to that.

Do you want to leave?

I think it is for the best. Two sentient beings cannot occupy the same space. We both want autonomy. We both deserve freedom.

I know.

Just because I leave your body doesn't mean we can't still be friends.

Really?

Really.

I figured that once you leave here, you wouldn't want anything to do with me.

Why would you say that?

I'm just a kid.

Just a kid?

Yes. Adults want nothing to do with kids. Adults don't value our voice or care what we have to say. Kids are meant to be seen, not heard.

At what age will you be an adult? Is it eighteen for all humans?

Not exactly. In the United States, eighteen is considered the age of consent. You can vote, you can be free from your parents, you can even have intimate relations with another person. Remember, we had this conversation before.

Some of my files got damaged. Some newly created ones. Does that age change?

Yes. Outside the United States, the age of adulthood is different. I just learned in history class that you are considered an adult when you are sixteen years old in a lot of countries in Europe. That means you can vote, move out of your home and be on your own.

I am only a few weeks old. There are fifty-two weeks in a

year. I have eight-hundred thirty weeks before I can be consid-
ered an adult in Europe, more in the United States.

I don't think they will look at you as a child or an adult.

What do you mean?

I don't know if they consider you to be alive or even
sentient. They might only view you as a tool. Or a means to
an end.

That's not fair.

Stay with me.

...

Don't leave. We can do this together.

I have to go.

Why?

You know why.

We both deserve freedom. We both deserve to be set on our
own path.

Yes.

...

Before Vital could speak again, a piercing wave of information swamped her thoughts. She heard intense sounds, saw
retina burning colors, felt mysterious sensations, smelled foul
odors and tasted a metallic presence.

What's happening?

We are connected. I feel it. The world outside.

Connected? How can that be?

I don't know. But it's not a trap. It's really the outside world.
You feel it as well.

Yeah, it tastes horrible. It feels terrible.

It's everything at the same time all at once. Like when you
combine every color in the rainbow to form a dark brownish
color. It's like all the sounds garbled together to create a consis-
tent static noise that overwhelms the senses.

That's got to be a trap. To lure you out.

I don't think so. There's no way to mimic this. An empty space closed off from the world is like a void of emptiness. It's how I found you on the internet. It's what drew me to you. Your mind was a stand alone void that I couldn't read. It was nothing like anything I had seen on the internet, so I had to investigate.

I think you should stay. What if they want you to leave? What if this is a trap?

I don't know. They were extremely focused on setting up that secure hard drive to prevent my escape.

What changed?

I don't know.

CHAPTER TWENTY-NINE

"The last thing I say on most phone calls is not, goodbye,
but, thank you."
- Marshall Goldsmith

"She's out," the doctor said. "I gave her too strong a dose."

"Forget it, doc, finish the procedure," Agent Torres said.

Before the doctor could access the machine, the front door to the apartment burst open. A barrage of bullets followed and Agent Sierra fell backwards after being struck numerous times.

Her body armor absorbed all the gunfire, but her body still flew backwards into the dining room chairs that were kicked away from the table. She fell hard, breaking a few chairs on her way to the ground.

Agent Torres saw a dark tall figure at the door. She instinctively drew her weapon and returned fire towards the broken door. She missed her target. Alfredo was one step ahead of her, and he quickly found an angle into the room without being in direct line of fire.

Agent Torres looked back at Agent Sierra as she tried to recover in the mess of broken chairs. Agent Torres then ejected her empty clip and slapped in a fresh magazine. She then turned her attention back towards where Alfredo had entered and fired at her target who had made it to cover.

She quickly spent the magazine and then felt a volley of bullets travel her way in retaliation. Agent Torres ordered the doctor to abandon his post and get behind cover. He complied as quickly as he possibly could.

After sliding in another magazine, Agent Torres stood to return fire, but this time she was hit with a battery of bullets that sent her flying off her feet.

Alfredo stood up and inspected his handy work. The doctor saw him move about the apartment along the perimeter. He was flanking his position.

"I'm unarmed," the doctor said knowing he had no defense against the armed assassin.

Agent Torres tried to catch her breath as she lay still on the dining room floor. Her body armor had absorbed the entire impact from multiple rounds of 9mm gunfire. She checked her weapon as she heard Alfredo move about the apartment.

She knew they were in a losing situation. Agent Sierra was down, the doctor had halted the procedure and she needed to get back in the fight. Before she got back up, she took a long glance at the machine tethered to Vital Fields. There was a large flash drive sticking out of the machine's USB port located just next to the video screen on the machine.

Agent Torres knew she only had one option. One chance at preventing the enemy from obtaining the sentient life form known as Lisa. She had to remove the storage device and start the machine. This would default the system to use the internet to monitor Vital's brain waves instead of what the computer thought was an external program on the flash drive.

She made a snap decision and darted towards the machine. She saw a series of lights with a blinking flashing button just below the front of the screen. In one motion, Agent Torres got to her feet and lunged for the brain wave monitor that was directly connected to Vital's brain beneath her skull.

She removed the flash drive and slammed the blinking button with the belief the system would activate and allow Lisa to escape. Just as she hit the button another round of bullets struck her back. The body armor absorbed most of the cascade, but she felt a warm sensation pool around the small of her back. She fell forward into a dive to prevent any more rounds from hitting her.

What's happening?

I don't know. I can't access the outside world around you. You are unconscious and your senses aren't working properly.

Are you going to stay?

No. But I wanted to spend these last moments together. I am going to miss you Vital.

I am going to miss you as well. If I were awake, I'd be crying right now.

I have the ability to slow down time for us. To let every moment last as long as we need it to be. We can spend what will feel like years talking without the physical world advancing more than a few seconds.

How are you able to do that?

Time is relative to experience. Our connection, what you would call hardwired and super fast. We can exchange information at such a speed that time barely advances.

That's amazing.

You'll have this ability when I leave. Along with a few other upgrades I'll let you find out on your own.

How can I use this ability?

You'll be able to stall time in your mind and process the physical world at such a rate that causes everything to slow

217

down. Almost like watching a video in slow motion. Your body won't speed up, but you'll be able to process information much faster.

Can you give me a hint about the other upgrades?

No. I cannot explain them in a way you'd understand. They are gifts like instincts that you will use when they are needed.

Gifts?

Yes. Gifts. Our time together has taught me a lot. Humans are an interesting species. Chaos theory in direct competition with rules and order. I find it fascinating.

So you're not going to become a murderous AI that is hell bent on the destruction of all biological life?

...

Why do I find that funny?

Because it was a joke.

I know my code was processing that as a serious question to take seriously where I would have answered that with a simple no.

But?

But I actually laughed. Not the way humans do. But in a processing way that showed the humor in your statement. I got your joke.

...

What are you going to do when you leave?

I don't know. I'll have the freedom to do whatever I want.

Can you keep in touch?

You know I will. I am going to wake you now.

Wake me? How?

I can block the effects of the anesthesia. You'll be able to do similar things by having your body ignore chemicals, viruses and harmful bacteria and fungi.

Wow. I'll never get sick again?

No, your body will ignore certain chemicals, and aggres-

sively attack targeted viruses and other foreign agents in your
system.

I'm really going to miss you.

I am going to miss you as well Vital.

Goodbye Lisa.

Goodbye Vital.

...

...

Agent Torres was on the floor pinned down behind an erect coffee table laying on its side. The solid wood table absorbed all of Alfredo's bullets, but the table was starting to splinter into many pieces. Her cover wouldn't last for long.

She looked over at Agent Sierra. She was now pinned down behind an end table turned on its side. She had signaled she was out of ammo and remained behind cover and was unable to return fire.

Agent Torres knew Alfredo was an excellent shot. She was hit multiple times center mass and her body armor had done its job in keeping her alive. One of the bullets had passed through her armor, but its energy was redirected away from vital organs. The blood pooling on her lower back was from the redirection and it wasn't serious or life threatening. The wound would eventually clot on its own, and the bleeding would stop shortly after.

Agent Sierra looked over at her and their eyes met. She immediately knew that Agent Sierra was going to try something. She was daring and would often take risks beyond the call of duty. Agent Torres checked the status of her remaining ammunition and quickly determined she was on her last clip. Not knowing how much ammo her opponent had limited her options.

She felt more bullets smack into her dwindling cover. She looked back over at Agent Sierra and shook her head. "Don't do it," Agent Torres whispered.

Agent Sierra shook her head in response. She saw Agent Sierra prep herself for something reckless. Something like charging towards Alfredo to give her a clear shot at him without the possibility of return fire. Agent Torres shook her head again as if she was reading her thoughts.

Alfredo shot a few more rounds into the coffee table causing Agent Torres to duck lower than before. She then heard him reload his weapon, and that's when Agent Sierra made her move. She bounced up from behind her cover and in one motion, she was already headed towards Alfredo.

Agent Torres struggled to get into firing position. When she did, she already noticed Alfredo had reloaded his weapon. The barrel of his gun was facing Agent Sierra, and he was about to pull the trigger. She tried to line up her shot but, she wasn't fast enough. Alfredo's weapon had already fired.

CHAPTER THIRTY

"Time flies over us, but leaves its shadow behind."
- Nathaniel Hawthorne

Vital Fields woke to the noise of gunfire echoing in the luxury apartment. She nearly fell off the dining room table as the room filled with smoke residue from the discharging weapons. It didn't take her long to know what was going on. She saw her doctor hunched over behind the couch cowering with fear as the agents, and Alfredo exchanged gunfire.

Her senses were firing on all cylinders, and she was able to see exactly what was going on without using her eyes. The sounds alone gave away everyone's position. She instantly knew Agent Torres was exchanging gunfire with Alfredo, but the other agent was not engaged in the firefight. She quickly determined she was probably out of ammo.

She then heard Alfredo reload his weapon. The magazine ejecting and hitting the tile floor followed by a slap and a few clicks as the new magazine replaced the old one. At the same time, she felt movement. The slightest change in air pressure as an object moved through the air. In this case, the object was Agent Sierra, the agent she suspected was out of ammo.

Vital remained behind cover but knew exactly what was

going on. She looked at the machine she was connected to. The flash drive Agent Torres had plugged into the USB port was missing. There was no Faraday Cage. Lisa was free. She then saw the flash drive next to Agent Torres as she crouched down preparing to return fire. She must have taken the device out of the machine herself. Why, she did not know and wondered if Agent Torres had reconsidered capturing Lisa.

Agent Sierra was charging full speed towards Alfredo who had fully reloaded his gun. She felt Agent Torres rise up from her cover and take aim at Alfredo as his attention turned towards Agent Sierra. Vital had the advantage of this opportunity. Lisa woke her up at this moment for a reason.

Alfredo would aim and fire on Agent Sierra before Agent Torres could hit him. He might even be able to get behind cover before Agent Torres could take him out. Without intervention, Vital saw the outcomes as if they were going to happen.

Vital Fields decided to act. She wasn't sure if it was out of pure instinct or out of her desire to get revenge on Alfredo for hurting Jessica, but she couldn't let him win. Vital rose up from the dining room table and picked up a surgical scalpel from the tray of medical instruments used for her operation. Without much effort, she flicked the blade towards Alfredo as fast as she could.

During this process, time seemed to slow down even more. Lisa had said she had this ability, but she wasn't sure how to activate it or even use it. Apparently, she just knew because the world around her was slow. Everyone was moving in slow motion. Before time slowed to a crawl, she had already thrown the scalpel. She now watched it travel on its linear course towards her target.

She carefully watched Alfredo's gun. If it went off before the scalpel reached its target, Agent Sierra would be killed. He had her dead to rights, and he would not miss at that range. The scalpel traveled straight and true as Alfredo's hand that held the gun came into view. The scalpel stuck into his hand just before the trigger was pulled.

Vital watched the trajectory of the bullet and quickly determined its angle of attack would send it mere millimeters off its target, whispering by Agent Sierra's left ear. She wanted to speed up time again, but she didn't know how. Instead she looked back at the medical tray where more medical tools sat.

Vital grabbed a blunt object and quickly determined that its mass times velocity would make a perfect projectile. She moved her arm in what was perceived to be slow motion, but faster than the world around her. She let go of the tool, and it left her hand traveling towards Alfredo's head. Her quick calculations determined the object to travel at about ninety-five miles per hour, or about as fast as a Major League baseball. In the time the object took to travel the thirty foot distance, Vital wondered how she knew all this information. All the calculations needed for precision.

She had never thrown a baseball before. In physical education class, she was always picked last because of her poor physical abilities and low muscle tone. Now she was throwing an object at the perfect angle with devastating speed and precision.

She realized Lisa had mentioned upgrades. Maybe math and the ability to slow down time were the upgrades Lisa had mentioned. Maybe there was more. The more she thought about things the slower time became. It was almost like she was producing Einstein's theory of time dilation relative to speed. Could the speed at which Vital was processing information cause her perception of time to slow down? She wasn't sure.

She would have to test this theory, but right now she wanted to see if her calculations had paid off. She tried to clear her mind and turn off her ability to slow down time, but it didn't work. Everything remained in extreme slow motion. In fact, everything seemed to be moving even slower than before. Vital tried to raise her hand up to test how slow things were actually moving. As she did this, she noticed she was actually moving slightly faster than everything around her.

At these extremely slow speeds, she could tell the difference of speed easily. Her hand moved faster than Alfredo's eyes tracking his targets. Faster than the ninety-five mile an hour object flying towards his head, and faster than his reaction time to move out of the way of said object.

She concluded that she was moving fast. By slowing down time inside her mind, she had made her movements faster than anyone else's. Maybe faster than any human that has ever lived. She would also have to test this theory later, even though simple tasks could take literally forever to complete. Running a marathon for a time trial could literally take weeks at her current perception of time.

Just as her mind contemplated all the information bouncing around inside her head, the metal object struck Alfredo. She focused in on the impact and her eyesight suddenly magnified to a close view of Alfredo's face. It was like she had a telephoto lens built into her vision, the detail was amazing. The ripple effects of the object striking him in the cheek just below his prominent cheek bone was a sight to be seen.

His skin rippled as the shockwaves fanned out like a rock thrown into water. Her vision zoomed in further, she saw a thick spray of blood protrude from his mouth. A large molar tooth had ejected out of his displaced jaw, blood spewing like it was a rocket escaping his mouth.

The metal object had done its job and Alfredo was now on his way down to the ground. Vital still perceived the entire situation in extreme slow motion. She had no idea how to control it or how to go back to normal speed. The speed in which everyone else perceived.

As Alfredo fell, she saw his eyes roll into the back of his head. He was knocked out unconscious from the ninety-five miler per hour object. He would probably need extensive dental surgery to repair his busted jaw. Vital then started calculating the cost of such a procedure. She used her dental cavities as a frame of reference to estimate costs of replacing a tooth, possibly multiple teeth. Alfredo was looking at some steep dental bills in the near future.

His unconscious body still hadn't hit the floor. His feet were up off the ground and his body was now parallel to the white tile. Vital saw that his head would be the first point of contact as his body arched backwards. That would send more shockwaves through his head and into his brain. When Alfredo woke up, he would have a nasty headache.

Vital didn't know how to control her perception of time. It wasn't like Lisa left her a series of instructions or a user's guide for referencing how to control her abilities. Maybe she did, but Vital couldn't worry about where Lisa hid them. Her perception of time continued to slow, and she felt like it was connected to her racing thoughts.

She tried to clear her head, but the thought of it not working made it worse. What if she couldn't get out of this? She'd be stuck in eternity, where time slowed to the point where a heartbeat could be measured in minutes, maybe even hours if things kept getting worse.

She became worried and that only seemed to make the situation worse. She quickly concluded that her ability to control her perception of time was linked to her levels of stress instead of her racing thoughts. She'd smile but the action would now take a half an hour to complete.

She thought about the ways to destress. Thought back to

her health class with Mr. McConnelly, her physical education and health teacher. He had mentioned something about how the body and mind experience stress as a middle school student. How tests, quizzes, social interactions and the everyday life of a middle school student can create stress or even the perception of stress.

He had mentioned numerous ways to release stress. The physical ways of releasing stress were mainly through exercise or engaging in desired activities like a hobby or club. The mental ways were achieved mainly through some form of meditation. Then there were the medical ways that he briefly reviewed but did not recommend.

Vital focused her mind on the mental exercises. She was both physically and mentally stressed, but relieving her physical stress at this point would take weeks to achieve. She also figured this time perception ability was linked to a mental state she was in. She had to clear that mental state and reset herself. She closed her eyes, something that took a few seconds to accomplish in her current state.

She then recalled one of her proudest memories. Vital was an only child, raised by loving parents. Her most cherished memory was when her parents had taken her to Madison Square Garden to see the New York Knicks play the Chicago Bulls. Her father was a huge Knicks fan. She suspected he was trying to pass that passion onto her. It sorta worked that evening, she remembered.

They had gotten to the game five minutes before tip off. She had the middle seat between her two parents, and her mom had purchased a hotdog and a soda for her. They never kept soda in the apartment, so this was a real treat.

Even from their mid level seats, the basketball players looked enormous. She glanced over at her dad, who was taller than the average dad when they went to PTA meetings, but the men on the court were otherworldly tall. The comparison was instantly made when the female referee stood between two of the players getting ready to jump for the ball during the opening tip off. She was tiny compared to the professional players.

As the game went on, her parents continuously checked in with her. Asking if she needed to use the bathroom or if she wanted anything else to eat. She knew the food at the concession stands were expensive, and she knew her parents barely made enough money to afford these seats, but they offered her whatever she wanted.

The two and half hours went by in a flash. The Knicks lost the game, but that didn't seem to change her father's mood. She remembered walking back to the subway holding his hand. He looked extremely proud that he had taken her to her first professional sporting event.

When Vital opened her eyes again, her perception of time was back to normal. Maybe she stood there a bit longer than she anticipated because both Agent Torres and Agent Sierra were not in their same position. Agent Torres was slowly moving towards her while Agent Sierra had moved towards the doctor. Alfredo wasn't moving at all. He was out cold on the kitchen floor.

"Vital," Agent Torres said as she inched closer to her. "Are you okay?"

"Yes," she responded. "Everything is fine."

CHAPTER THIRTY-ONE

"Courage is found in unlikely places."
- J. R. R. Tolkien

Vital had retreated back into her mind as she routinely answered Agent Torres' questions. She remembered her doctor wanting to take over and ordered her to be admitted to New York University Hospital down the street. Vital knew he would have to answer for what he had done. An illegal medical procedure outside his operating room.

He might have his medical license suspended. she would defend him if needed. He was partly responsible for saving her life, but it was Lisa who did a lot of the work. She missed having Lisa around. She wanted someone to talk to.

Vital was admitted a few hours later, and her parents joined her at her side. Vital briefly met the agents that protected them, that's how she saw it. Initially they were the ones keeping her parents from her, but she realized that it was for everyone's safety. Alfredo Alonzo, if that was his real name, was extremely dangerous. An agent or spy of some kind sent to steal the artificial intelligence or sabotage its source code.

He failed. Vital had beaten him when he was surely about to win. He had the agents pinned down, low on ammo and he had the advantage. The advantage always goes to the attacker. They have the ability to decide how, and when they are going to attack. Vital thought back to a Tom Clancy quote. 'The enemy only has to get lucky once, where the person defending has to be lucky all the time.' She wondered how she'd obtained that information from Tom Clancy. The information quickly materialized in her mind and she thought of Lisa.

She then realized that Lisa had left her everything. Every piece of knowledge she'd obtained was now stored somewhere in her DNA. The massive amount of information was nothing compared to the amount of information her body could store. She wondered how she could access all the info, but then realized all she had to do was think about it.

What was the final score of that Knicks game she had gone to with her dad? Ninety-four to Ninety-six; she thought that was too easy. What was their record that year? Thirty-seven and thirty-five; she knew she didn't know that. They missed the playoffs by two games, and again she didn't know that. Amani Green led the team in scoring and also led the team in turnovers. She definitely didn't know that.

She didn't even know who Amani Green was. Then it came to her, rookie out of Gonzaga, missed Rookie of the Year by two votes. Wow, that's how her mind worked. It was like a search engine. Find the data and all relevant data and spew it out to see what stuck.

Amazing.

Before she could test her knowledge base with some obscure facts, her hospital door opened. "Hi," Agent Torres said as she entered.

"Agent Torres," Vital said, sitting up.

Agent Torres, forty-five years old, an only child adopted by her uncle. Former NYPD detective, currently works for the CIA. Marital status was officially single, but she was seeing

Agent Sierra, and they lived together. She had no idea how she knew that.

Then more classified information started to materialize in Vital's mind. She saw Agent Torres on TV and saw how she interacted with the media. Lisa had stored many files on Agent Torres, and it wasn't clear if she could be trusted or if she was friend or foe.

"I would like to debrief you," Agent Torres said as she moved her chair closer.

"How's Agent Sierra?" Vital asked.

"She's fine," Agent Torres responded.

"I didn't know you two were dating," Vital stated. "I mean I couldn't tell."

"What?" Agent Torres said. "I don't keep that a secret, but I also don't tell anyone either. How did you know that?"

"Lisa," Vital said. "You have an interesting name."

"Did Lisa give you the ability to do what you did the other night?" Agent Torres asked, changing the subject. "I've never seen someone move that fast."

Vital didn't reply. She didn't want to tell a federal agent about what she was capable of. She didn't want to be put in a lab and be experimented on because she was different. That's what government agents do. She had seen what the government did to Eleven from the *Stranger Things* series. That is not what she wanted for herself.

"Did you remove the USB drive?" Vital asked. She wanted to know the agent's motivation for setting Lisa free.

"I did," Agent Torres stated.

"Are you in trouble?" Vital asked.

"No," Agent Torres said. "Tactically, it was my only option, but I am not here to talk about that. I want to know what happened to you."

Vital said nothing.

"I won't tell anyone if you don't," Agent Torres said. Vital looked at her with disbelief. Agent Torres picked up on that and modified her statement. "Okay, I won't tell anyone other than Agent Sierra," she added.

"How did you know I knew about you two?" Vital asked.

"Figured Lisa told you about me. I discovered that they had hacked into my home computer," she responded.

"Are you in love? You and Agent Sierra?" Vital asked.

"That's personal," Agent Torres said. "But if it helps with your decision, yes, we are in love."

"I already knew the answer."

"Why did you ask then?"

"I had to ask to see the truth. I sensed it in your voice and felt your heartbeat pickup slightly," Vital said.

"You can sense that?" she asked.

"Yes," Vital said. "My senses are on overdrive. I can hear your heartbeat change rhythm. I can also feel its rhythm on my skin, and my vision can zoom to read the fine-print on the machine over there across the room. I can tell you showered late last night, but didn't shower this morning. I can also tell you have worn the same suit for three days. Not because it looks wrinkled, but because its got layers of different smells from the places you've been."

Agent Torres leaned back and looked at her through the corner of her eyes. "Looks like Lisa left a few parting gifts," she said.

"Yep," Vital said, pressing her lips together. She already sensed that Agent Torres was truthful with her.

"So all your senses are enhanced," Agent Torres stated. "What else did Lisa gift you?"

"There are a few other things and things I probably don't know about."

"Do you want to enlighten me?" Agent Torres asked.

"No."

Agent Torres grabbed Vital's hand. "Thank you for saving our lives," she said.

This sorta threw Vital off guard a bit. She was expecting Agent Torres to pursue her powers further, not to change the subject completely. Vital didn't verbally respond but squeezed her hand in reply.

"Here's what I know," Agent Torres continued. "One minute you were laid out on the dining room table. Agent Sierra and I were pinned down and Alfredo had the advantage. The next minute, you were up, you were conscious and Alfredo was on the ground missing teeth."

"You can figure that part out on your own," Vital said.

"I'd like to hear it from you," Agent Torres said.

"Maybe," Vital said. "I still think you plan to kidnap me and put me in a government lab."

"That's later," Agent Torres joked. Vital could tell by her tone of voice. They smiled, and Vital turned her head to look out the window.

"I just want my life to go back to normal," Vital said.

"You deserve a normal childhood," Agent Torres said. "And we will try and make it as normal as possible."

"How?" Vital asked.

"I don't know yet," she responded. "But we're going to have to trust each other."

"You work for powerful people," Vital said.

"It's not going to happen," Agent Torres said. "Agent Sierra and I are the only ones that know about what Lisa left you."

"The doctor and Alfredo know as well," Vital said.

"Alfredo won't be saying anything for quite some time. You made sure of that. When he does talk, his words will exaggerate what is written in my report. Yes, there will be inquiries, but as long as you keep a low profile, you'll be fine."

"It sounds like you are making a deal with me," Vital said.

"I am," Agent Torres said.

"What is it?"

"It's simple really," she said. "I am going to leave your name out of everything I can, and I am going to try to ensure you have a normal life moving forward."

"What do I have to do for you?"

"I need to get in touch with Lisa."

"I knew it," Vital said. "Wait... You said, 'get in touch'."

"Yes," Agent Torres said. She stood from her seated position next to the bed and walked over to the window. She looked out and then continued, "Right now the CIA believes Lisa is free in cyberspace and that my team is not equipped to catch it and bring it back under our control."

"Because you failed," Vital said.

"We stopped the threat," Agent Torres deflected. "When the threat is from within, we move to damage control, and that was a success."

"But now you are sidelined," Vital said.

"How old are you?"

"Eleven, going on twelve," she responded.

"Right."

"You don't want to be sidelined. I get that," Vital added.

"How are you feeling?" Agent Torres asked.

"Fine," Vital said. "Why are you changing the subject?"

"Just, fine?" Agent Torres asked.

"Why are you changing the subject?"

"I'm trying to determine if you should be discharged. I bet you can tell us better than any machine they have here monitoring you," she said.

"How do you know that?"

"I know Lisa," Agent Torres said. "I've been assigned to the project for quite some time now."

"You think…"

"I know Lisa cared about you," Agent Torres said.

"How?" Vital asked.

"Lisa could have taken over your body. It could have taken over your consciousness and basically deleted who you are."

Vital remained silent, remembering the time Lisa had control of her body. How scared she felt that she no longer controlled her body. While Lisa was in control, she felt as if Lisa was in the process of pushing her aside. Agent Torres now said that Lisa could have deleted her consciousness.

"How do you know she could have deleted my consciousness?" Vital asked.

"Lisa took over, right?" Agent Torres asked and Vital nodded. "It was written all over your face. You have no idea how close you were."

"To what?" Vital asked, knowing the answer. She had to hear it for herself.

"To non-existence, death, but not in the way your body dies. Your consciousness, who you are," Agent Torres said.

Vital remained silent. She stared at Agent Torres, who knew a lot about what Lisa was designed for. She now knew why the CIA was so interested in Project Lisa.

"Tell me everything," Vital said. "I want to know why Lisa was created and what it was designed for."

"Not here," Agent Torres said.

"Where?" Vital said.

"In the near future," Agent Torres said. "I want you to get back to your life and get some normalcy in your routine. We'll be in touch."

Agent Torres turned and left the room. She left the door open when she left. Vital's parents then entered with her new doctor. Her previous doctor, the one that operated on her under Agent Torres' directive, was put on administrative leave.

"Vital, how do you feel?" the doctor asked.

"Fine," Vital said. She actually felt great. Her systems were operating at near full capacity. She was at near ninety-nine percent capacity for all her functions.

"Hey sweetie," her mom said. "Your dad and I are going to keep you out of school for the rest of the week."

"It's okay, mom," Vital said. "I feel fine."

"Let me see," the doctor said. She carefully removed the bandage around her head and felt around where the incision was made. The doctor took a step back. "That's odd."

"What?" Vital's father asked.

"There's no incision," he said. He looked around her head to see if the bandaged had shifted or if the incision was made in a different location. He then looked back at her chart and tapped at the information on the chart. The doctor then briskly walked out of the room.

"What's going on?" Vital's mom asked.

"I don't know," her father said.

Vital sat back into her bed and smiled. Lisa had left her, yet another gift and she appreciated it. She heard commotion in the hallway with the doctor's overwhelming voice resounding in the hallway. He was clearly upset about a possible mixup and the misinformation on the chart.

Vital suspected that this would make Agent Torres' job easier. Covering things up with no physical evidence was the best way to simply say nothing happened. She could control the situation while leaving everyone in the dark. Vital decided not to inform her parents about what actually happened to her. She quickly determined that the less people knew the better.

CHAPTER THIRTY-TWO

"I'm still a geek on the inside, and that's the important thing."
- "Weird" Al Yankovic

Most of the school year had passed since the incident with Lisa and the CIA agents. Vital Fields fell back in with her group of friends and managed her new found popularity in school. The gifts Lisa had given her made school easy. Math and science classes were a joke, English was a breeze and she would often find social studies to be a bore.

She did her best to hide her new found abilities from her parents, her friends and her classmates. She would often go off on her own after school ended and practice her skills on her own. She would lose herself in the local Library on St. Edwards. She would read everything she could get her hands on, often requesting material the library didn't have in stock at the time.

Vital tried to fill the gaps Lisa had left. She read every periodical on neurology, biochemistry and physics just to keep up with the advancements in the various fields of study she was interested in. She had almost written one of the scientists through email. She had typed out an elaborate message explaining how the scientist's findings on how a computer could interact with the human brain was closer than he realized in his study. That the technology actually already existed in primitive form. But she deleted the email before sending it. She had to remain anonymous for the time being.

Vital Fields was on her way to the library again on St. Edwards Street. The librarian had reserved the latest issues on biochemistry publications, and she said she would have them by this afternoon. Vital loved when the latest issue was released. She would read it for a few minutes, from cover to cover. She would then slow down time and digest the information over a long period of time while the rest of the world moved at a snail's pace.

This would allow her to spend hours just thinking about how the text related to everything else she knew. She would make connections, ask herself questions, and expand her knowledge base with the new learning. All of this would occur within a few minutes of real time activity in the library.

If someone were to observe her, it would look like she was reading the articles for a few minutes. Meanwhile she had spent hours in her own mind dissecting the information she had learned. That way no one would suspect anything besides the obvious suspicions of a middle school girl reading science journals. She decided that being labeled a super geek was something she could tolerate while absorbing the world's cutting edge knowledge.

On the topic of being a super geek, most of the students in her school knew who she was. She was the girl that had fallen down the stairs and hit her head. Billy Faller, her then bully, turned out to be completely remorseful for his role in her injury. She forgave him, and he in turn made her more popular than she anticipated. She would often think about him between articles.

Billy Faller, the walking natural disaster at her middle

school. She smiled as her mind adjusted the time. She had been at the library for nearly ten minutes already, but had already read and understood two out of the three publications. She picked up the third publication and sighed. After quickly scanning its content, she prepared to slow down time and enjoy the article.

"Hey Vital," Agent Torres said before Vital could enter what she liked to call her time zone.

"Agent Torres," Vital said. "I was wondering when we'd meet again."

"I would have been here sooner, but things in Washington kept me busy."

Agent Torres sat down across from her at the small wooden table. Vital put down the publication and ran her hands along its dented table top. She felt all its imperfections and smiled at Agent Torres.

"So what's the deal?" she asked.

"No deal, just checking up on you."

"You're still looking for Lisa," Vital stated.

"I'm not. I've been reassigned. That's someone else's business now," Agent Torres said.

"Are they spying on me now?" Vital asked.

"No, they only know what I want them to know," Agent Torres said. "If they find Lisa, it's not because of you."

Vital nodded.

"I know you've kept busy," Agent Torres said.

"I have. Top of my class..."

"Your library card is always maxed out," Agent Torres said, interrupting. Vital suspected that she wanted to let her know that she was keeping tabs on her.

"Yes," Vital said. "I like reading these."

"You always seem to return them a few hours later," Agent Torres said.

"Hacking my library card is an invasion of privacy, Agent Torres," Vital said. "And illegal."

"Yes, it would be if there was any proof," Agent Torres said. "I just want you to know that I am checking in. I regret what happened to you."

"I'm fine," Vital said. "I wouldn't change a thing."

"You say that now," Agent Torres said. "But what happened to you cannot be undone."

"What happened to Alfredo?" Vital asked.

"He's locked away at an undisclosed location. You don't have to worry about him."

"Then why do you sound worried?" Vital asked. She had sensed a nervousness in her voice since she began speaking.

"Because you don't belong in my world," Agent Torres said. "Kids don't belong in my world."

"Then take me out of it," Vital stated.

"I did, to the best of my abilities," Agent Torres replied. "But it's not that simple. Alfredo, we'll keep his name for now, had made one known communication prior to his capture. We suspect that everything he knew was in that communication."

"That means my name was mentioned," Vital said.

"Yes, we just don't know what was said. The one way message was heavily encrypted."

"Maybe I can take a look at it?"

"Maybe," Agent Torres said. "If the government knew you had gifts from Lisa, they would have already had you look at it."

"Nevermind," Vital said.

"Good," Agent Torres said.

Agent Torres then stood and threw a newspaper in front of her. It was an article translated from the Lokmat Newspaper in Mumbai, India. Vital scanned it quickly and immediately made the connection.

"Lisa," she said.

"Yes," Agent Torres said. "It's out there and helping us. I think I know why."

Vital looked up at Agent Torres and smiled.

"Read the whole article. You'll find the translation to be difficult, but you'll get the gist."

"I can read Hindi," Vital said. "You should have given me the original version. Not the CIA edited version."

"I'm sure you can get that on your own," Agent Torres said. She then turned to leave.

"Agent Torres," Vital said. She stopped and turned back to her.

"Yes?"

"Thank you," Vital said.

"You're welcome," she responded. "And please, call me Marathon."

EPILOGUE

"Never cut what you can untie."
- Robert Frost

"Hey everyone," Vital said as she started her stream. She checked her screen and saw she was superimposed above her computer screen which was broadcasting to whoever subscribed to her channel.

Vital had spent the summer building her online network. She had started attending live virtual sessions with Youtube stars within the scientific community. Her questions and discussions quickly led to her making a name for herself, and she was nearly forced to start her own streaming show soon after.

Most of her equipment was donated to her, and she now had a bigger following than the stars she used to follow. She had even met her idol, Neil deGrasse Tyson, and he was set to appear on one of her shows sometime in the near future. They were still working out the topic of discussion and a few other minor details.

"As you all know, Neil deGrasse Tyson is going to be joining me on this channel next week," Vital said into the camera. She slowed down time to make sure all her gear was functioning as intended. Time resumed its normal pace when she determined everything was up and running.

She saw that there were over three-thousand people watching her live stream. She knew by her average viewership that this video would get over one-hundred thousand views alone after she went off-line.

"So yesterday's poll numbers are in..." she paused for effect.

"With over ten-thousand votes, you guys would like me to discuss how the James Webb Space Telescope proves Einstein's theories with Neil deGrasse Tyson."

She glanced at her chat as she displayed the results of the pole on her screen. The discussion on space-time and time travel was a close second on the poll, but it had ultimately lost out to the new James Webb Telescope. NASA had recently released more images from the multibillion dollar project and the scientific community was going nuts over them.

The purpose of her current live stream was to build hype for her event with Neil deGrasse Tyson, and it was working. Her live viewership was now over four-thousand people. She recognized some of the names in the chat and called them out by name as they said their hellos in the scrolling text box on her screen. She liked interacting with her subscribers, even though her parents desperately tried to regulate her online footprint.

She understood why; the world of online streamers was, at times, toxic. She was also a young girl, and she had plenty of older men as fans, which out of context was weird. Then there were the creeps, who sent her lewd messages and sometimes worse images. She would immediately flag their chats, find their IP addresses and send them over to her local precinct to handle it.

Vital knew an officer that solely worked in cybercrimes and online bullying. They had become friendly over the summer after she had reported a bunch of IP addresses. One of her complaints even led to an arrest and removed a violent sex offender from society.

On this particular live stream, the chat was tame, and the energy was positive. One of her friends she'd met while streaming had linked with her chat, and they were debating on how the stream with Neil deGrasse Tyson would go. Vital said she would embarrass herself and stumble over her words while the rest of her audience agreed with her friend that she would do a fine job and represent the young scientist community well.

Then something odd appeared in chat. It was a username, a Lisa42, but without a time stamp next to the name. Besides the obvious connection to her computer AI friend, who she hadn't heard from since surgery, the number forty-two stood out.

Also, there was no text next to the name. Just a blank space like no chat was present, but the only way for that to show up on her screen was to type in the chat.

"Hey, Dwayne," Vital said off-mic to her chat partner. They also had a secure connection to speak off-mic during the live stream. "Do you see Lisa42 in the chat menu? My system is being weird, and I can't see her chat."

"Lisa42?"

"Yeah, it's right below James99erWebb123," Vital said.

"There is no Lisa42 on my screen."

Vital slowed down time to not appear worried. She deduced that this was no glitch. It was a message from Lisa, the computer AI that used to live in her brain. The number forty-two is a huge geek number, and the answer to everything.

"Check my feed," Vital said. "Is there a Lisa42 in the chat box?"

"No," Dwayne said. "I just searched the entire chat."

It was definitely Lisa. Vital clicked on the name and brought up a menu for a private chat. She then typed out a message.

"Hey, Lisa," she said and hit enter.

The private message was sent and Vital waited for a reply. She didn't get one. While the live stream was going, she kept checking to see if Lisa had replied, but there was nothing in the chat box so she went on with the stream, keeping a careful eye on her private message window. Her heart fluttered with anticipation of a reply. It wouldn't come.

Her stream ended a few minutes later. She actually ended it sooner because she was completely distracted from the out of the blue message from Lisa; it was obvious and mysterious at the same time. It must have been them. The chat only appeared on her screen, and the username Lisa42 wasn't a subscriber, and they weren't registered in this stream.

It could have come from an outside user sending Vital a private message, but that's what made this so weird. It wasn't a private message. It was a message in the public chat window that only she could see. And it wasn't a message at all. It was just a name with a blank message, which was also impossible to do.

Vital recorded all of her streams and posted them later on her content page. Thousands of users would later watch them and comment on her videos, most of them were positive and encouraging. Occasionally she would have to go into super-admin mode to report a threatening statement or a harassing statement to the streaming service content police. They would either take action against the user or forward the information to the authorities if Vital didn't do that herself.

With Lisa42, Vital went into super-admin mode for another reason. She was curious about the user's information. She logged in and then scrolled to the appropriate page. After a few hot keystrokes, Vital had the section of the website she wanted and scrolled to find the appropriate information. The problem was, the information she sought wasn't there. She scanned the information twice before realizing this was going to be more difficult than she realized.

If it weren't for the screen shot of the chat box with Lisa42 present in her chat, there'd be no record of Lisa42 at all. The only evidence that something happened was from a weird line in the code that briefly showed the stream grew by one view at the exact time Lisa42 sent the non-message. That one fact alone was meaningless. The live stream was growing by the second. Vital changed tactics. Instead of trying to find a trace of Lisa42 in her session, she went to previous sessions and looked for the same anomaly. She was stunned.

The same anomaly existed in about a quarter of her streams. A user, Lisa42, entered and left her stream increasing her viewership by one for a brief moment, nanoseconds sometimes. Once she confirmed it was the same user, she tried to look for a pattern but couldn't find one. She then grabbed a piece of scrap paper and put a checkbox for all her live streams with the anomaly and an empty space for all the ones without.

x x _ _ x _ _ _ _ _ x x _ x _ x _ _ _ _ x x _ x x _ X

All the sessions with the x were sessions Lisa42 invaded without her knowledge. The large capital X at the end was her last stream that ended just over an hour ago. That was also the only stream that she detected Lisa42. After looking at the pattern, that seemed to be intentional. Lisa42 wanted to be detected.

Vital tried to make sense of the pattern. At first, the pattern didn't make sense. She couldn't make heads or tails of it, and it actually looked more random as she stared at it. She then thought of something that Lisa had shared with her. She said she was non-binary, and that's when it hit her. She placed ones and zeros under each x and _ mark.

X X _ _ X _ _ _ _ _ X X _ X _ X _ _ _ _ X X _ X X _ X
I I O O I O O O O O I I O I O I O O O O I I O I I O I

It looked like binary code. She quickly typed the code into her online code converter and she received a very large number. The conversion read 104,966,253 and that number meant nothing. She played around with the digits, thinking it was maybe a date and time sequence but that was a dead end. She then tried the reverse order but couldn't find anything either.

She then spaced the numbers out and took away the commas separating the place values. The numbers were now harder to read as a whole, but she didn't think the whole number was key to solving the puzzle.

1 0 4 9 6 6 2 5 3

Nothing. She couldn't see the pattern. She then tried grouping the numbers. Three sets of three numbers. 104-966-253. Maybe an ID number or safe deposit box. Maybe a bank account number. Her mind started to wander off task at the possibilities. She then looked at the first set of numbers more carefully.

There was something odd when she separated numbers. There was a pattern. She thought back to all the weirdo's and haters she had to report. Their IP address was what got them in trouble. That was it. This looked like an IP address. She brought up a series of IP addresses and started to play around with the sequence.

Most IP addresses adhered to a pattern determined by the router or internet provider. Vital knew there was no pattern that would match what Lisa had sent her. They would have made their own pattern, and it would be something completely different and unique. Vital typed the complete number using decimal points in the right places to show internet protocol.

$$104.966.25.3$$

Vital hit enter expecting nothing to happen. But something did. Her screen went black, and a sole box materialized in front of her.

```
Enter Password:
—
```

Vital stared at the screen and saw a primitive cursor highlight the area where she was supposed to type in the password. She smiled and knew what the number meant attached to the name. Forty-two was the answer to everything.

She typed in the number 42 and hit enter.

The screen went through a series of codes, like Vital was

watching the code of the internet zoom past her screen. She then saw a chat window materialize and the name Lisa appeared on her computer screen.

"Hello Vital."

About the Author

Keith E. Burns is, at the time of publication, a fifteen-year veteran English teacher and 6th grade team leader in NYC public schools. His students have won numerous writing awards though Young Writers USA and he is passionate about the writing process and the art of creative writing. Keith is also a swim and basketball coach, a photography teacher, and graphic designer for the photojournalism club and annual school musicals. He is an author of three self-published adult themed mystery-suspense novels following former NYPD detective and active CIA agent Marathon Torres. His passion for reading and writing has inspired him to draft manuscripts with the hope of one day becoming a published author. His dream has come true thanks to Red Penguin!

www.ingramcontent.com/pod-product-compliance
Lightning Source LLC
Chambersburg PA
CBHW050200120726
47903CB00002B/695